*mic
thy inspiration
love,
Lindi*

Uptown Flirt

by

Lindi Peterson

Cover designer: Lynnette Bonner
Indie Cover Designs
Cover images: Dreamstime xl 46562897
Dreamstime l 19725434
Dreamstime l 37659878

Editor Emily Sewell

Love Atlanta Style reality show boasts "love is hotter in the south."

Once a year Atlanta heats up when one bachelor meets ten ladies. At the end of the show only one lady will capture his heart. But there are nine other ladies. These nine ladies from season one—Grace, Suzanna, Riley, Vivian, Farrah, Claudine, Sadie, Kimmie, and Audrey—have stories, too.

And they need to be told.

Book 2. Uptown Flirt—Suzanna's story.

Dedication

To Lindi's Lovin' Love Readers Group. You rock and know how to make a girl feel special. Each and every one of you makes me smile. Thank you for hanging in there with me.

CHAPTER ONE

REALLY?

Who gets dumped by two guys in one night?

Suzanna Worth, apparently. Why me?

The craziness that is my life surrounds me as I sit at a high top in a popular bar in the Buckhead area of Atlanta. The hip, vibrant atmosphere fades as I'm in a bit of shock after Peter met me here as planned, bought me a martini, then told me he was through. Relationships weren't for him, he said before kissing the top of my hand. Then he walked off.

Didn't give me any sort of rebuttal opportunity.

Even the placard with the fun tropical drinks seems to mock me.

I hadn't had time to process his actions and words when my phone indicated I had a text. I did smile when I saw it was from Gray.

Until I read it.

Hi. You're great. But I can't hang with you anymore. Sorry to do this by text.

Two dates in one night.

1

And they're both gone within five minutes of each other.

I wish the producers of Love Atlanta Style, the reality show I was on not too long ago, would start a bachelorette show. At least the guys leave weekly, not every five minutes.

I don't normally plan two dates in one night, but Peter had told me he could only do before-dinner drinks tonight. He had another obligation that started at seven. A work thing, he told me.

So I contacted Gray who said he'd be thrilled to meet me and hang out at an engagement party I'm supposed to attend tonight at another popular hangout down the street. That party starts at eight o'clock. It sounded like an okay plan. Drinks with Peter. Dinner and party with Gray.

Especially since I'm not serious with either one of them. Peter has barely kissed me goodnight while Gray has only kissed me on the cheek. But they're both fun, single, and not interested in a long-term relationship.

Like me.

Long-term equals no term. At least in my book. My idea of giving long-term a try was being on the reality show Love Atlanta Style. True to form, that didn't work

2

either. I was the fifth girl to be asked to leave. To go home alone.

And now I sit here alone.

My phone beeps with another text. Since I have no more dates that can dump me tonight, I look. My father.

Great.

I open the text. I don't let my heart become too excited as his words. The more-absent-than-not Jameson Worth is coming to visit in one week. More than likely he's coming to Atlanta for business and will take me to a couple of quick meals in between his meetings and dinners.

That is if he even shows up. I can't count how many times these upcoming visits have been canceled or postponed. It's how I've lived my life with my father. I've come to expect nothing from him. Monetarily, emotionally, or fatherly.

And he'll ask me about my employment. That's one area he's had an interest in ever since I was on Love Atlanta Style. He was opposed to me doing the show. He thought if I had a decent job, no reality show could pull me from it. At least I'll have something to tell him in the job area. Something I haven't told anyone.

I text a quick "can't wait to see you" message. Good thing texts don't mirror facial expressions. And no, even though there is an emoji that has my exact doubtful feeling, I'm not texting it to my father. Even if I did, he probably wouldn't understand it.

The time on my phone says five forty-five. Grace and Justin will be here in fifteen minutes. I can't sit here without a date. Not in front of them. Grace and I met on Love Atlanta Style. We were both vying for bachelor Cole. He chose Peggy, but Grace and I became good friends. And we became friends with Riley, too. She can't make it tonight, canceled at the last minute, but we are having a girls shopping trip tomorrow.

Back to my current dilemma. Grace, hotel heiress, has just found her true love, Justin. She's so in love. I'm happy for her.

Tonight was going to be special. I was going to tell her about my new job. But being dumped by two guys in one night would totally contradict the job news. Actually makes the news kind of unbelievable.

The news might have to wait.

Grace told me dating Peter and Gray at the same time wouldn't work. She also said it was a disaster in the making. She started calling me Uptown Flirt since we hang out in Buckhead, the uptown part of Atlanta. Justin had nicknamed her Uptown Heiress and she'd been trying to think of a similar nickname for me.

I balked at the nickname and assured her I had everything under control. And I thought I did. To sit here and tell her I have no idea what happened seems impossible. Seems like I'm admitting something but I'm not sure what.

I'm not ready to admit this double failure to Grace.

Not yet.

And I'm not ready to sit here without a date.

Maybe I should leave.

I look toward the entrance and I see her. She's beautiful with her dark brown hair and amazing smile. Justin, who's easy on the eyes himself, leans down and gives her a kiss on the cheek. She smiles at him and wraps her arm around his neck for a moment. They kiss again.

Ugh. Dread seeps through me. I don't want to sit here alone with my friend and a guy that I'm sure will be proposing to her soon. I can't look like the failure that I am. There's no way to escape, though.

Looking to my right I see a guy about to walk by me. He's built, dressed in an expensive looking gray suit. A crisp white shirt and a maroon and gray striped tie complete his attire. And he isn't wearing a ring. I tap him on the arm. "Excuse me."

He stops. "Yes?"

I look up. So he's wearing glasses. Black-rimmed glasses. I realize how crazy this idea really is and I am about to let him go. Then I see his eyes. Gorgeous blue eyes hidden behind the lenses almost leave me at a loss for words. Almost.

There's no time for that, though.

His face is amazingly handsome, his hair a color between light brown and blond, thick, yet cut short. If I tell the truth his glasses make him look sexy in a smart kind of way.

I glance toward the entrance. A shift in the crowd indicates Grace and Justin are on their way. I quickly stand and step in front of the guy in the suit. "I'll give you a hundred dollars if you sit here for an hour and pretend to be my date." Did I just say that?

"What?"

I see Grace and Justin making their way through a throng of people. "Please? Help a girl out? A desperate girl?" I sit down, patting the empty stool. Even though Grace will know this isn't Peter or Gray, at least I won't be dateless.

I must look desperate because he awkwardly slides onto the barstool next to me. I look at him. "I'm Suzanna. Wow. My friend will never believe I'm dating someone so studious looking."

I probably shouldn't have said that out loud. But he is totally not my type of guy. All of my types are sitting with girls.

"Nathan." He slides his glasses off. "Do I look less studious now?"

My heart pings slightly at this new look. "Why, yes you do."

"They'll stay off for an extra fifty dollars."

Surprise and shock work together to form a smile. "Deal."

As I finish speaking, Grace and Justin arrive. "Hello." Grace gives me a hug before sitting.

Nathan stands briefly and nods at Grace as he and Justin shake hands. I notice Nathan grasping his glasses in his other hand which he is keeping out of sight.

"Grace, Justin, this is Nathan. Nathan, these are my friends."

A few hellos make their way across the table.

Grace raises her brows at me when the guys aren't looking, nodding toward Nathan who she knows isn't Peter or Gray.

She'll just have to wonder.

I just hope she doesn't think I'm dating three guys. That simply crosses the line.

After the waiter takes our drink orders I grab Grace's hand. "So how are things? You look great. Both of you do."

She stares at Justin for a moment before she responds. "Everything is great. And with you?"

I don't think about looking at Nathan before I respond. "Good. How is your business going?" I ask Grace. Before she can answer I turn to Nathan. "Grace and Justin just opened a yacht restoration business."

"That sounds interesting," Nathan says.

"It is." Justin nods toward Nathan. "Your line of work?"

Nathan smiles. Curiosity flows through me. What does Nathan do?

"I'm a financial planner."

I'm glad I don't have anything in my mouth because I probably would have spit it out. Financial planner?

Seriously? But of course. He's so dressed the part. I shouldn't be surprised at all. But I bet Grace is.

Now I know he for sure he's not my type of guy.

"That's awesome." Grace looks at Nathan. "How did you meet Suzanna?"

Nathan's gaze darts toward me. It lingers and I find myself lost in his blue eyes for a moment. I wonder how much he can see. Can he see my bluish-green eyes? My lips with their pretty pink lipstick that's guaranteed to stay on for hours?

"I guess you can say we kind of ran into each other." Smiling that gorgeous smile, he looks back at Justin and Grace. "How did you two meet?"

Kudos to Nathan for taking the focus off us. I want to squeeze his hands, but I'd probably break his glasses.

"I was her father's employee and she felt sorry for me." Justin winks at Grace.

"Don't listen to him. He did work for my father, but there is no feeling sorry for him. He's a good guy that can make his own way in the world. He asked me to coffee one night, and the rest is history, as they say."

Justin leans back as the waiter sets our drinks on the table. "Fun story to tell the grandkids. This girl got on my bike without even knowing my name."

"She must like coffee," Nathan says, his fingers wrapping around his shot of whiskey.

We all laugh. So Nathan does have a sense of humor behind his brainiac job and black-rimmed glasses.

As we all take a sip of our drinks, I almost choke on my martini. A guy who could be Nathan's twin is walking toward our table.

Except he's not wearing glasses. Like Nathan, he's dressed extremely well but in a more casual way. Tailored black slacks, a sky-blue button up that accentuates those truly blue eyes, and like Nathan, he's not wearing a ring.

I guess I'm staring, because he stares back at me. Then he looks at Nathan. Then he looks back at me. Watching his eyes is like watching a tennis match.

But then he stops. Walking, not looking.

"Nathan? I'm not used to seeing you—"

"In a club after work," Nathan interjects before shaking hands with him. "I'm going to be joining you a little while."

He leaves it at that while I'm wondering like crazy who this new man is.

The new man takes charge. "I'm Ned Parks. Nathan's brother. Twin brother as if that isn't obvious." Ned offers his hand to Justin.

10

Justin shakes Ned's hand. "Justin Walker. And this is Grace Adams. I'm sure you already know Suzanna." Justin nods toward me.

"So great to see you, Ned." I look at him with what I hope are pleading eyes. Pleading for him to go along with me and my crazy scheme. Of which he knows nothing.

"Nice to see you?" His cadence is slow, his tone questioning. Maybe Justin and Grace won't pick up on it. "I take it you'll be joining us shortly, as well?"

"She will." Nathan grabs my hand. I can't deny I'm surprised and touched. Can he sense how much I want to impress Grace and Justin? Impress isn't the right word, really. More like saving face against what Grace assured me was a bad idea.

She was right, of course.

I need to quit being so impulsive.

But as Nathan's hand still holds mine I think impulsive isn't always bad.

Then I look at Ned. Nicely dressed, yet not overdressed. He seems at home in this pulsing place. Nice body. No ring.

Feeling totally wrong about obsessing over Ned while holding Nathan's hand, I pull my hand away from Nathan's, hoping guilt doesn't show on my face.

Of course he has no way of knowing I'm feeling guilty.

About his brother.

Twin brother.

I try not to make it obvious, but my gaze follows Ned as he walks to a table not far from ours. He's instantly surrounded by people, females.

Of course.

In moments Ned is no longer visible amongst the pretty dresses, gorgeous hair, and long legs.

Smiling, I turn back to our party and find every eye on me.

"Is everything okay, Suzanna?" Grace's expression shows concern. Her eyes are saying "are you crazy?"

Buying a moment of reprieve and hoping the drink will calm me, I take a sip. The cool taste makes me forget Nathan, Ned and my good news that I now can't share with anyone.

How can I tell Grace that the girl who was dumped by two guys in one night grabbed a total stranger to pose as her date, then shifted gears the minute said stranger's twin brother showed up, is now the voice behind the Love Atlanta Style Twitter dating handle?

CHAPTER TWO

"SURE. EVERYTHING'S FINE." I see by Grace's expression that she doesn't believe me. But that's okay. I need to push through this night, figure out how to work my way over to Ned, and go from there.

Farrah's engagement party is at a restaurant down the street, but I don't think I'm going to make it. I've got research to do.

"Nathan, your brother seems nice. What does he do? Is he into numbers like you?" Grace asks.

Nathan laughs. "Ned? Numbers? Not unless he's counting women. He runs his own business. A dating service."

Another spewing-drink moment so soon? Seriously? Can this get any better? Meeting Ned is now a necessity, not a want. This is crazy. I look upward like I might see some angels playing their harps waxing love songs over my head. And life.

But no, dimmed lights and a ceiling are all that meet my gaze.

And six questioning eyes as I look around the table.

13

Oh, yeah. I do have a real life situation happening right now. Backing my brain up, away from perfect Ned and his perfect occupation, I concentrate on the people in front of me.

And on Nathan sitting next to me. Glasses still in his lap. Financial planner still his occupation.

"Dating service? That must be an interesting job. I'm sure Suzanna told you we met filming Love Atlanta Style. Dating in front of millions," Grace says.

I look at Nathan to see his reaction. It's calm. But then I think he's a calm kind of guy. Things like that probably don't faze him.

"It's not as glamorous as it sounds, Ned's job. It's a small business. A start-up, actually. I advised him to invest his money in something more stable, but he declined."

He totally ignores the Love Atlanta Style information Grace delivered. He is mighty good at diverting. Or he doesn't believe in finding love like that. You know, on television.

Grace cranes her neck to look around me. "He's surrounded by females, that's for sure."

We all look at Ned. Some of us look longer than others.

The urge to join that party is about to overtake me.

But that would be so impolite.

"It's almost time to head to Farrah's party. Are you about ready?" Grace asks.

Farrah was also on Love Atlanta Style. Grace, Riley and I have remained friends now almost two years after our season finished. We see the other girls at certain events and have even cultivated pseudo relationships with some of them. Since we were all on Love Atlanta Style looking for love, we were having sort of a minireunion at Farrah's engagement party.

I'll simply grab the highlights from Grace. "Actually, I've decided not to go. It's going to be crazy there. And well, I want to hang out with this guy," I tap Nathan on the arm, "for a while. Quiet like. Not party crazy like. Tell me all about it tomorrow?"

Grace looks at me like she knows I'm up to something, but she has no idea what. We'll chat tomorrow during our shopping trip with Riley.

"I'm going to try to not be mad at you ditching us. I'll see you at eleven at Phipps, right? Nordstrom?"

"I'll be there."

"Good." Grace opens her clutch purse that she has set on the table. She pulls out her phone, glances down, swipes her finger across the front then frowns. "Geez. This is crazy." Grace looks at me. "The LAS Twitter has really ramped things up and it's going crazy."

I swallow hard. This is the perfect segue. The perfect invitation to tell her I'm the new voice behind the LAS Twitter handle. Words that are stuck in my throat refuse to come out. Why can't I tell her?

Them?

All of them?

They're all staring at me. "Crazy?"

She shoves her phone back in her purse. "Yes. The advice has gotten off the wall. Over the top I guess. It's pretty amusing now."

I suddenly wish I had Nathan's hand in mine to hold onto. To feel grounded. Secure.

Amusing?

I thought my advice was spot on. My boss, Sonny, who worked with all of us on LAS, has given me nothing but kudos all week. He said followers were up. The web page hits are up. Tremendously.

Amusing?

Grace and Justin stand. "I may have to give the LAS crew a call and ask them who they have running that handle. It's probably half the guys on the production

16

team. They're probably too cheap to pay someone after they let go that drama diva they had hired to do it last year." Grace shakes her head.

I couldn't speak now even if I had too. Grace hugs me, then Nathan. Justin shakes Nathan's hand then waves goodbye to me before sliding some cash on the table.

"See you tomorrow." Grace narrows her eyes at me. "I'll give Farrah some excuse why you aren't at her engagement party."

"Thanks. I owe you." My mind swirls with thoughts and concerns. Nathan and Ned. Grace's criticism about the Twitter account. I walked into this bar secure, confident, and excited.

It has taken me almost one hour to feel confused, conflicted, and crazy.

NATHAN AND I have migrated to Ned's crowd and have been hanging out for about twenty minutes. I've pushed the job thoughts to the back of my mind. Sonny thinks I'm doing great and that's all that matters.

Nathan has put his glasses on. The crowd assumes we are together.

So does Ned, I'm sure.

I need to correct this misunderstanding.

And the opportunity presents itself when Nathan excuses himself to go and buy me another martini. Even though two is my limit I said yes to his offer hoping for some alone time with Ned.

To capture his attention I need to make my way through the female admirers that surround him. Actually this shouldn't be a problem. I don't have a problem with men. Normally. But this night has been anything but normal.

"Excuse me." I tap a redhead on the arm. As she turns I slide my way in front of her. I hear her huff. She has no choice but to acknowledge my slick takeover of her space.

"Hello, Susan." Ned's voice carries my attention away from the disappointed redhead to see if he's talking to me. Surely handsome, charismatic Ned didn't forget my name.

But he did. He's looking straight at me, waiting for a response. I don't think this has ever happened before, a man forgetting my name. "It's Suzanna."

Ned takes a drink of his golden cocktail. "Ah, yes. Suzanne. Pardon my mistake."

I smile through blood that's about to boil. "Suzanna. *Uh*."

"How about I just call you "baby." That's easy to remember."

"Suzanna's good." I smile as I speak and wonder why I'm interested in capturing this man's attention. Oh, yeah. Good looking, social job, charismatic. That's my type of guy.

Right?

I went on Love Atlanta Style hoping to gain the attention of the bachelor. That didn't work. Now, shame on Grace for finding her right guy and teasing me with it. Not intentionally of course. Her happiness with Justin just goes to show me that Mr. Right can come along at any time.

Even when you are least expecting it.

But he should at least be able to remember your name, I think.

"So, how long have you been hanging out with Nathan?"

Ned's eyes are blue like Nathan's, but for some reason they look different. Maybe they're unfiltered as Ned doesn't wear glasses.

I turn slightly and see a gorgeous brunette making her way through the crowd.

But to give Ned credit, his gaze doesn't linger too long on her. He turns his attention to me.

"I just met Nathan tonight. Here." A sigh of relief escapes as I can see Nathan still at the bar. But I probably don't have much time to capture Ned's attention. I need to work fast. And smart. "He was nice enough to help me out of a jam."

"What kind of a jam could a beautiful woman like you be in?"

His words melt everything inside of me. "Nothing dramatic. To be honest I was saving face in front of my friend. She had given me advice that I didn't follow. Turns out she was right, but I didn't want her to know that she was right."

His eyebrows raise. "She's a good friend?"

"The best."

"Maybe you'll take her advice the next time then."

I shrug. "Maybe. But if I had I wouldn't have met you." I smile my coy smile.

He nods. "Or Nathan. Here he comes with your drink."

Nathan is weaving his way through the throng of females. His suit and tie look out of place against the backdrop of pulsing music, loud conversation, and fancy drink glasses. The style is staid and conservative compared to this crowd. I'm surprised my gaze wants to linger longer on Nathan as he comes closer to me. My head is telling me Ned is talking to me, but my ears aren't listening.

". . .family picnic tomorrow." Now my head does turn at the use of the words family and tomorrow. Did he just ask me to go to a family event? I haven't known him ten minutes.

I guess I still can make an impression.

Even if it did take him three tries to get my name right.

"Excuse me?" Nathan will be at my side in seconds, so if Ned is asking me out he better hurry.

"I said I'm surprised Nathan is out tonight. Normally he's at home working. And I'm not sure he's even coming to our family picnic tomorrow."

Disappointment jets through me at the lack of an invitation. "Oh, really? Why?"

"Why what?" Nathan asks as he hands me my drink.

"I was just telling your beautiful date that you are usually at home working during the evening and you have been known to miss a family picnic or two because of work. But here you are. Out. Drinking, no less. Her beauty has already made you a changed man."

"It's club soda with lime. Don't get too excited about your little brother breaking his mold."

He speaks with confidence. I find I like that. "Little brother? I thought you were twins."

Ned nods. "I managed to push my way out first. Minutes before slowpoke here." He now nods toward Nathan.

"Saving the best for last." Nathan takes a sip of his nonalcoholic drink as his eyelids shut briefly over his gorgeous blue eyes. Once again I find my attention lingering on Nathan.

But he's so not my type.

Laughter grabs my attention. Ned's casual demeanor and easiness entice me and I shift my weight from Nathan toward Ned, hoping he can read body language.

But Ned has been captivated by the redhead again. Her long manicured fingers gently touch his shirt, caress his forearm. And yes, caress is the most appropriate word.

And her voice? Her conversation caresses him as well. It appears I'm not on his radar anymore.

Shoving disappointment down, I refuse to step away and lose my real estate next to Ned.

"So, my brother's caught you in his web?"

Nathan's few words speak volume in terms of Ned's character. A character I should stay away from, but instead it calls to me like a siren's song. And I'm always crashing on the shore, waves pounding. But I continue to dive in for more.

The thought strikes me that this is fabulous research for my new job. Grace's words refuse to stay planted in my mind. I can't let her influence what I write. I'll be upfront with Nathan and tell him what I'm doing. He's a nice guy and deserves to know the truth.

"It's not what you think." I smile, hoping to entice his interest.

"Really? Then what is it?"

I think it's time I trust someone with my secret.

And that someone is Nathan.

CHAPTER THREE

"I HAVE A new job." I sip my drink.

"That's great. At least by your smile and tone I think you think it's great."

Slowly twirling the stemmed glass between my fingers, I keep an eye on Ned. Ned who is content with the redhead for the moment.

Longer than a moment, actually, but I can't let that bother me. "It's a good thing. I enjoy it."

"And what does that have to do with Ned?" he asks.

"My job has to do with dating. And since Ned is a matchmaker, I think we can form an alliance."

Nathan moves closer. "Could you repeat that?"

The music has bumped up in volume, the song beating with heavy bass and drums. "I think Ned and I could benefit from each other business-wise."

Nathan nods, a bit of an unbelieving look on his face. Like he's heard it before.

"I'm serious." Why I feel the need to reiterate, I don't know. Nathan is not the man I'm trying to catch.

"It's okay." Nathan nods toward Ned. "I'm used to this. All the girls always want to date Ned. I'm simply their vehicle to him."

Nathan's words unsettle my heart. Even though he has just stated my plan, it sounds shameful and sad coming from him.

Probably because it is shameful and sad. But I can't help who I'm attracted to. I'm made a certain way, attracted to a certain type of man. And financial-minded, business-suit wearing, always-working men aren't my type. Even if their eyes are an ocean-blue color and their body fills the suit perfectly. "You shouldn't sell yourself short."

"So you're standing your ground that you are interested in Ned for business reasons?"

It's not a lie. And Nathan didn't use the word only. "I would love to pick his brain about how he decides who goes together."

"Too bad you're not free tomorrow. We're having a family picnic. If you didn't already have plans with your friends, you could come with me." He looks at me, like my expression might influence his next words. "To pick Ned's brain, of course."

My luck is unbelievable. "I can skip the shopping. No big deal."

Nathan half-smiles and I'm intrigued.

Again.

His black-framed glasses can only hold so much nerdy weight when there are beautiful eyes and a dazzling smile to go along with them.

"You're a spontaneous woman, Suzanna, willing to change plans when a better wind blows in your direction. Interesting."

Great. Now he thinks I'm wishy-washy and noncommittal. "I can see why you would say that, but I don't know Farrah, the gal that is throwing the engagement party tonight, all that well, and I can shop with Grace and Riley anytime."

"Ah," he says. "I understand. But it's the art of the commitment."

I tap the arm of his glasses. "You think too much."

"Not too much. I try to think smart."

"Have you smarted your way into uninviting me?"

He shakes his head. "No. You're still invited."

I breathe easily again. "Thank you. I'm sure I'll have a great time."

I LOVE MY new job. I can work any hours. Even at two in the morning when I can't sleep. And I can't sleep because I'm excited about tomorrow. I texted Grace and Riley that I wouldn't be joining them for our shopping trip. The only way I got away with this without too much grief is because I told them I had to work.

And that's the truth.

I'm going to glean dating advice info from the man who knows enough to run a dating service. The fact that I'll be escorted by his brainy brother is no big deal. But that's okay. Nathan is easy on the eyes as well, even if his eyes are only viewable behind thick lenses.

I spent my early twenties doing HR work. But then I landed the gig on Love Atlanta Style and the nine-to-five life flew out the window. I had offered to do HR for Grace and Justin's yacht restoration company, but they are keeping it simple regarding employees. They have two. Grace and Justin.

I've been able to live off the income I received from Love Atlanta Style and the rogue appearances I've done for the show, but finances are starting to look lean. So when Sonny from LAS approached me about this job, I couldn't imagine anything more perfect.

27

And it will ease my dad's mind. I think I've seen him once since I was on Love Atlanta Style. He didn't approve of me being on the show. Maybe if he'd had more input in the past twenty-eight years of my life, I might listen to him now. But he chose to divorce my mom when I was two, and he's flitted in and out of my life at his convenience.

His company is always in the way. My mom lives a fabulous life across the country in California. She's never remarried, but she's retired and has a lot of friends.

So while I would love to see Dad if he does show up, I'm not counting on it.

My phone beeps indicating the battery is low. I plug it into its charger. My job can be worked from my phone. But hey, I can't be on twenty-four seven. I started last week with my notifications turned on, but my phone constantly beeped, buzzed, or sang. Over the week I've tried out every sound possible with the same result.

They are all irritating when they're heard every minute of the day. That might be an exaggeration, but not by much.

I settle into my bed with my tablet and call up my Twitter account. Part of the challenge is giving advice in the limited word count allowed. Sonny said I did a great job on the test scenarios. Then there's the blog where I'll start writing columns in about a month. There's an art and a style to the column they want to uphold, so a gal named Eunice is going to be training me on that starting next week.

Grace's words about my advice being over the top float through my mind. I can't let them bother me. I can only do this job the best I know how. And Sonny is paying me a good salary to keep this handle lively and fun.

Even at two a.m.

Any confidence I may have lost after being dumped twice in one evening was replaced when I met Nathan, then subsequently, Ned. The date master. Whom I will be spending tomorrow afternoon with. Nathan is picking me up at noon.

I answer a couple of tweets with some more advice, hoping someone in the city finds love tonight. Scrolling back through my responses, I'm suddenly second-guessing everything I've tweeted.

I need to stop. Grace is my friend, but Sonny is my boss. And he thinks I'm doing well so far. But the nagging feeling that Grace might talk to Sonny won't go away. I just need to tell her it's me giving the advice.

We'll have a great laugh about it, she'll say the advice isn't that over the top, and we'll still be besties.

At least that's how I hope it goes down.

IF MY FAMILY ever had a family picnic, which we won't, I would have the Parks plan it. We are north of Atlanta in Talking Rock at Chateau Meichtry. A winery. The Parks have taken over this wonderful place for the afternoon. Rolling hills, vineyards, and a quaint tasting room are nestled in this beautiful location. Nathan and I find a parking spot.

"Here we are. The Parks family picnic."

"This place is beautiful."

"It is. There's not too many of us, which is why we can hold our event here." He exits the car and opens my car door, his hand ready to help me out. I place my hand in his, and purposefully ignore the perfect fit and the gentleness with which he pulls me toward him, the slight brush of his fingers before he lets go.

The door shuts softly behind me, a testament to the level of luxury of Nathan's car. So not what I expected from him. I thought he'd have a more practical ride.

Now I'm thinking too much.

Enjoy the moment.

Look for Ned.

But as we walk to the back of the car, the trunk pops open.

Nathan nods to a small cooler. "Our contribution." He grabs the cooler, which has a pull handle and wheels, then the trunk shuts. Instead of wheeling the cooler across the gravel parking lot, he carries it. It's then I notice his arms. His biceps.

He must work out.

The edges of his baby blue polo sleeves hug his forearm in a way that draws attention. I also notice his tapered waist. His polo is tucked into khaki shorts. His belt is brown and matches his shoes.

"Ready to meet the Parks?"

I look at his face, his eyes seemingly a lighter blue than last night. Maybe it's the sunny May day. Maybe it's the sky with its puffy white clouds hanging abstractly in the aqua expanse. Or are they a reflection of his shirt? Maybe his lenses make them look more amazing than they really are. "Sure. Ready."

We walk a short distance to where about ten people are gathered. Ornate tables and a stone patio greet us as looks of surprise come our way as well. It then becomes a flurry of hellos and hugs. Names are being given to me that I hope I don't have to remember later. The last woman to hug Nathan is elegant, classy, and beautiful.

"Mom." Nathan greets her before giving her a hug. He holds onto her a bit longer than he did the aunts and female cousins.

"Nathan." She gives him a kiss on the cheek then turns her attention to me. "Hello. My, aren't you lovely. Nathan, have you been holding out on your mother?"

He sets the cooler down before draping his arm around his mother's shoulder. "No. I haven't been holding out. This is my friend, Suzanna. Suzanna, this is my mom, Catherine Parks."

I shake hands with his very elegant mother. "It's nice to meet you, Mrs. Parks."

"Please call me Cat. Everyone else does. It's a pleasure to meet you. How long have you known Nathan?"

Somehow to say not even twenty-four hours doesn't seem appropriate.

"I met Suzanna at a party not too long ago." Nathan's quick wit and the way he puts words together give his mother a truthful yet vague answer.

"And was it love at first sight?"

Nathan now looks at me before turning his attention back to his mother. "I'm not sure. Suzanna?"

"We haven't mentioned the L word yet," I quickly interject. I watch as two of the women take the cooler and start setting out the food Nathan has packed.

Cat's eyes widen as she looks over my shoulder. "Ned's here. And he's alone. Again." She looks at Nathan. "How is it your brother can run a dating service, but he can't find a date for himself?"

Interesting. Ned's truly on the market. It would be rude to turn and stare, so I don't.

"A date? Mom, he has twenty dates every night. You know that. He doesn't want to settle down."

Nathan's diatribe makes Ned sound like the party boy I met last night. Just the kind of guy I'm looking for. We can have some fun, take it slow.

Settle down eventually.

"Excuse me." Cat nods toward Ned.

My gaze naturally follows her, and I shift my position to watch her make her way to Ned. She reaches him before the rest of the crew and stands by her son's side as he charms all the females and shakes the hands of the other men.

As the crowd thins, Nathan taps my elbow, and we walk to Ned and Cat.

"Brother." Ned shakes Nathan's hand and they half hug. "Long time no see." He smiles.

Has Ned not noticed me, or is he playing a game?

His button up shirt is short-sleeved and tucked into his black shorts. He's built, I know he is, but as I shift my gaze between the brothers, it comes to my attention that Nathan must work out more than Ned. That's interesting.

Finally, as my gaze reaches Ned's face, he smiles and points at me. "Hi. I remember you. Sue. . .? Right?"

Embarrassment washes through me at my expectations. I swallow hard, trying to keep my voice cordial and void of irritation. "Suzann*a*." I can't help that last bit of snark.

"That's right. It's good to see you. I like that you have an interest in my brother. He doesn't go out much, and he won't take my dating advice."

"It seems he doesn't need your advice. Suzanna is lovely." Cat takes my hand in hers and I'm feeling all out of place. "I'm sure Nathan has told you of his father's love of a good wine. We always hold our little family picnics at a winery in his memory. He would have loved this one."

Nathan adjusts his glasses higher on his nose. His mother is still holding my hand and I have no idea what to say. I want to say that this information would be helpful and Nathan could have filled me in on the drive here. We were in the car over an hour.

"He would be a big fan of this place." Ned points to the table with the wine glasses. "Speaking of which, I'm going to grab a glass. Anyone else?"

"I'll join you." Cat lets go of my hand, and she and Ned walk away.

"That was awkward." The words slip out. I don't think I meant them to.

"I guess I should fill my mom in on why you are really here. That way she won't be disappointed when I don't bring you to the next family function."

His tone sounds regretful. This day is too perfect to be anything but perfect. Or maybe that is guilt I'm feeling. "Let's go and have some wine. Join the family."

"Start your research, you mean." He smiles, and we start toward the table. "Red or white," he asks.

"I like both. For this sunny fun day, I think I'll try a white. Not too sweet, though."

A pretty blonde stands behind the table and gives us a detailed description of each wine. After a short tasting, we each walk away with a glass of chardonnay to a table with snacks, plates, and napkins. Juggling our small plates and drinks, we make our way to a table where two ladies are sitting with Ned.

Nathan sets his plate and glass down then grabs a chair from another table. He motions for me to sit next to Ned, which I happily do. Nathan's chair is further away from me than Ned's. I wonder if this is noticeable to anyone but me.

Of course, I'm happy with this. Nathan is trying to help me out. But the slight breeze teases me with his cologne, and the sun highlights his blondish-brown hair.

"You can tell it's love," one of the aunts says. "She can't quit staring at him."

"Carol. Quit being so loud."

Carol shakes her head. "Don't pay Dolly any attention, dear. She's always talking about love. Looking for it, too."

We all laugh softly, and I pull my gaze from Nathan. Because of the seating, it's almost impossible for me to stare at Ned. That's probably a good thing.

"So, now that you've met the Parks clan, tell my Aunt Carol and Dolly about your family," Nathan says.

Nathan is very good at covering our situation. I take a breath. "There's not much to tell. I am an only child. My parents were only children, so there aren't a lot of us. My mom and dad divorced when I was two. That's about it."

"Do your parents live in Georgia?" Dolly asks.

"No. Mom lives in California, Dad is based in New York. He owns his own company and travels all over the world, though. I'm not ever sure where he is. Except he's coming here next week." As soon as I speak the words, I regret them. "Let me correct that. Dad texted that he was coming here. Until I see him I don't believe it."

And with those few words, I've summed up my dysfunctional relationship with my father to strangers. Oh, and a man I'm trying to impress.

My wine glass is still plenty full. It's not like the alcohol is talking.

"I'd say he's missing out if he doesn't show up." Nathan's words warm my heart.

Ned scrapes his chair across the concrete then stands. "Do you lovely ladies want any snacks?" His attention is focused on his aunts. He acts like I'm not sitting next to him.

"I'm good. Thank you, hon." Dolly nibbles on a cracker.

"Me, too." Carol nods toward her plate still covered in food.

"Cool." Ned pushes his chair up to the table. A sure sign he's not coming back.

I take a sip of my wine as I contemplate the Ned situation. Granted, he probably thinks I'm Nathan's date. But still, he could at least talk to me, right? No law against a brother speaking with his brother's girl. Not that I am his brother's girl.

My, this can become complicated.

I turn slightly toward the snack table. If Ned is alone, I may be in need of some more cheese. Before I can evaluate the situation, my phone chimes indicating I have a new text message.

Looking quickly, to make sure it's not my boss, I take a deep breath when I see it's from my father. I turn the face of my phone toward Nathan. "See. My father is texting me. He's probably already canceling his commitment for next week."

Nathan shakes his head. "Like I said, his loss."

I open the text, my eyes widening at the words.

"Uh, oh." Nathan laughs. "Did he reschedule?"

I reread the text before looking at Nathan. "He did. He's in Atlanta now and hopes I'm available for dinner."

CHAPTER FOUR

"THIS IS CRAZY. He thinks either I have no plans, or if I do, I'll drop them just because he comes into town." My finger hovers over my phone keyboard as I decide how to respond.

"What do you have going on tonight?" Nathan asks.

"I think it's sweet your father surprised you like this," Carol adds. "Make the most of it, dear."

"Yes." Dolly winks at me. "Make sure he pays, too."

"Aunt Dolly, behave." Nathan half smiles at her before turning his gaze to me. "What time do you need to get back? I don't want you to miss this opportunity to see your father."

Shaking my head, I text Dad. "I'll see where he wants to meet. This is crazy. I'm always having to change my plans to accommodate his schedule." I hit the send button then set my phone on the table.

Nathan takes my hand in his. "I can imagine that would be frustrating. Let's see what he has to say."

He gently squeezes my hand before letting go.

Loud male laughter erupts behind me, and I don't linger in the feel of Nathan's hand on mine. Instead I turn to find Ned conversing with his mom and a couple other ladies. They are all family, this I know, but he seems to attract a crowd wherever he goes. A female crowd.

The women are still smiling and giggling as Ned sips his wine. His tale must have been amusing. Our group is staring at my phone, like everything hinges on my father's response. Except Nathan isn't focused on my phone. He's focused on me.

I'm thankful I've pulled my crazy thick hair into a high ponytail as the shining sun makes the day slightly warm for this time of the year. My face is flushed, but I'm not sure if I should blame the sun, Nathan's attention, or Ned's lack of attention.

Of course, my father's craziness could be the culprit as well.

I'm at a beautiful winery, with two guys and an amazing family and I can't fully enjoy myself. I must have issues.

My phone chimes again. I quickly read the text. Out loud.

"We have reservations for three at six o'clock at Callaways. Bring a date. I'm sure you have one. Can't wait to see you. It's been too long."

If I thought I was flushed moments ago, it's nothing to how I'm feeling now. *Bring a date?* Seriously? This is too embarrassing.

"How considerate," Carol says. "See dear, he's thinking of you and your social life."

Dolly nods. "So true. Obviously he's trying to make up for bad behavior in the past. And how lucky for Nathan. You'll have a nice dinner as well as meeting Suzanna's father."

I smile, covering up my crazy beating heart. I have gotten myself in quite a situation. Of course, Nathan's family, who have no idea I want to connect with Ned, would assume Nathan would be going with me tonight.

"I already have plans tonight. Sorry."

Nathan's voice is all raspy and strong like he's forcing himself to speak the words.

I, on the other hand, am a little surprised, in not a good way, at his immediate dismissal of himself from my situation.

The wind whistles softly by, chilling the air slightly.

Or was it my situation that brought on the chill.

"I have an idea," Nathan says. "Why doesn't Ned go in my place? He'll have fun. Just explain to your father that I had a previous commitment, but my brother happened to be free. Would that work?"

Nothing had prepared me for Nathan's words.

Nor was I prepared for the disappointment when he spoke them.

"IS HE ALWAYS late?"

Ned's impatience is on my nerves. "I'm not sure. Always isn't often."

"What?"

His confused look doesn't draw me closer to him. It makes me want to wipe it off his face. I sigh. I'm not sure what I expected from this man who has everything that I think is important going for him. But I think I want to like him, right? I should be comfortable with him standing next to me. Honestly, when Nathan told me a free meal would convince Ned to come, I thought he was kidding.

But he wasn't.

Nathan.

His quiet, studious demeanor invades my thoughts and the noise in the atmospheric restaurant my father suggested fades.

"Suzanna. I'm sorry to have kept you waiting."

The strong, foreign scent of my father's cologne settles over me. I turn and give him a quick hug. Like Mom, he's not into hugging. "Good to see you."

He nods. "You, too."

We step back from each other. Dad looks like he always does. Silver hair, lean figure. His face indicates he's lived life but has lived it well.

"I'm Ned Parks."

Ned shoves his hand toward my father, who reciprocates. A hearty handshake between two men, neither of whom I know well.

"Jameson Worth. Glad you could join us tonight. I always enjoy meeting my little girl's friends."

The way he says "little girl's" causes me to shake my head and roll my eyes. I'm not and have never been his "little girl." But he plays the part of doting father well. Especially when he has someone to impress.

I look around him to see if he's brought someone.

He hasn't.

The hostess approaches and moments later we are seated at the back of the restaurant. Small talk of food and drinks occupy our conversation until the waiter takes our order and our menus. Now we all sit, me next to Ned, my father across the table.

"This place is a dream," Ned says. "Cool place to bring a date. I'll have to remember this. Although I'll have to figure out how to go Dutch. Pricey."

My father's eyes look like they want to bug out of his head while I try and process the words with some sort of understanding.

"Aren't you here with a date?" My father's voice, filled with undeniable tension, slices the air.

Ned holds his hands in the air. "I was only kidding. It was a joke."

Shoulders relax around the table. Well, the male shoulders relax. Mine have been tense since I left the vineyard in Ned's car. His ride is nice. More expensive than Nathan's actually, but it lacked warmth. A warmth I refused to attribute to personality and compatibility. Ned had the music blaring all the way here. I tried to start a conversation more than once to tell him about my job, but the words "this is one of my favorite songs" kept coming out of his mouth.

45

I should like Ned. He's my perfect guy. He has so many characteristics of the guy I want to date, while Nathan barely checks off any.

Yet Nathan pushes buttons that I didn't know I had.

But here I am. Surrounded by swank and unfamiliarity.

"So, what's my little girl been up to lately?"

Excitement courses through me. "I have a new job."

His eyebrows raise as he sips his drink. "Tell me about it."

"You remember that dating show I was on?"

Now his eyes roll as he shakes his head. "How could I forget?"

"Dad, stop. It was good for me. Anyway, they have hired me as the voice behind their Twitter handle."

"And?"

"I'm the one tweeting dating advice for all of Atlanta."

To say my father looks confused is an understatement. "So what is the job?"

Ned sets his drink down. "You tweet dating advice?"

My father points to Ned. "Why doesn't this young man know this about you? I thought this was your boyfriend."

The conversation din, the tinkling of forks against plates, even ice cubes rattling inside their glass cages combine into a roar. Add to that my father's words and Ned's incredulous look, and it all makes me want to run. Nathan's calm image comes into my mind.

Why?

"Ned is my date. That's different than a boyfriend."

Ned leans close to me. "Let's take a selfie and tweet that we're together. That will be great for my business." Why is it I don't have a desire to move closer to him? In fact I pull a half inch away from him as he snaps a picture with his phone.

"Perfect hot dates ATL is my Twitter handle. This is cool. We'll have to hang out more. We can help each other. Give me your cell number and I'll text this to you."

"Hang out more? I'm not following. I thought you two were together. You don't even have her phone number?" My father signals the waiter to bring another round of drinks.

Great. I haven't touched the wine in front of me. I know it's expensive, but I keep thinking of earlier today, sipping wine with Nathan. How comfortable I felt.

Of course it took spending time with Ned to realize this. I glance over at Ned and his drop-dead gorgeous face. My brain is on board with how great of a combination Ned and I are. It's my heart that is rebelling.

My phone indicates Ned's text has come through. I upload the picture with all the hashtags I'm required to use at the job. I never thought I'd have a job where I would be working during dinner. With family. On a date.

Date?

Wait. This isn't really a date.

I shove my phone into my purse, ready to spend some quality time with my dad. Ned is still scrolling on his phone.

"This is blowing up." Ned looks at me. "We are being retweeted every second. Cool." His index finger continues to move down the screen of his phone, while my dad can't contain his puzzled expression.

"I don't understand your generation. I probably never will. Your generation is probably the reason. . . Never mind."

So my "date" can't keep his head up long enough to converse and now Dad is talking in riddles. Great. Just how I envisioned a perfect Saturday night.

Mercifully, the waiter slides our plates in front of us. I think this will cause Ned to pocket his phone, but no, he simply sets it to the right of his plate and continues to scroll in between bites.

I have noticed a slew of gals refilling our water glasses, even when there is still plenty of water in them. Yes, Ned is *that* good looking. My father will probably ask me all sorts of crazy questions when we are alone, and I'll have no good answers.

Oh, well, I'll deal with that later.

Ned does manage to interject a "cool" or "excellent" every now and then as my father and I talk, but I am thankful when my father places his card in the black folder the waiter has brought. We can finally call this evening a night.

"I'll give you a call in the morning," Dad says. "We'll see about getting together sometime tomorrow. I'm not sure how long I'm in town."

"Sounds great." I wipe my lips with my napkin and place it on the table. It's all I can do not to place my purse in my lap. Not that Ned would notice. He's still looking at his phone.

Thankfully, I see the waiter approach, so I grab my purse, ready to leave as soon as Dad adds the tip and signs.

The waiter places the black folder on the table. "I'm sorry, Sir. There seems to be a problem with your card. It was declined."

CHAPTER FIVE

MY FATHER'S EYES widen. His gray eyebrows raise like eyes surprised at this news the waiter is imparting. Ned shifts uncomfortably next to me, but keeps his hands on the table as if to say "I'm not handing over my card."

Okay, that's probably totally unfair, but it's how I perceive his body language.

"That's unfortunate." My father takes the card out of the folder. "I'm suspecting some sort of identity theft fraud alert. It's happened before. All of my cards will be declined if that's the case. I'll make a call as soon as we leave and try to straighten out this mess. I do apologize."

His gaze is focused on the waiter. The waiter that he doesn't know, that he's never seen before in his life and more than likely will never see again. In the moments it takes my father to tuck the declined card back into his wallet, Ned doesn't make a move.

It only takes me seconds to place my credit card in the black folder, the waiter nodding at me before he walks off. If my father thinks it odd that Ned hasn't offered to pay, the declined card debacle probably keeps him from saying anything.

The awkward silence hovers until I sign the receipt for a dinner that has cost me more than three weeks of groceries. I could have bought a pair of shoes with the tip alone.

Trying to maintain an air of grace and nicety, I smile as I place my purse on my shoulder. "Are we ready?"

Both men scoot their chairs back, neither looking my way.

I walk out of the swanky restaurant, my head held high, while two men I barely know follow.

With quick hugs and murmurs of seeing each other soon, I ditch them both to Uber to my condo.

Alone.

It's only after the Uber driver turns the corner that I wonder if my father has cash, or if he'll end up walking back to his hotel.

I WAKE UP to three missed calls and three emails from my boss. Doesn't he realize it's Sunday morning? He doesn't state a matter at hand, but assuming it's urgent I turn my phone on speaker and call him as my Keurig spits and sputters its process of heating my water.

"How do you know Ned Parks and why didn't I know this information?" Sonny's baritone voice bellows through my small galley kitchen.

"Good morning to you, too." I'm not very good at keeping the snark at bay before I've had coffee. Plus, he wants to talk about Ned. Really?

"Suzanna. This is crucial information you've been keeping from me. What else haven't you told me?"

"My father's credit card was declined at dinner last night and I'm due to start my period tomorrow. And it's Sunday morning. Sunday. What else do you want to know?" I watch my coffee cup fill with the strong brew I obviously need to communicate. My period? Really?

Sonny chuckles. "Sorry I'm bothering you on a Sunday, but I wouldn't have called you if it wasn't important. Crucial, actually. I've booked an event for you and Ned. This is genius you knowing him. The two dating guru's of Atlanta hanging out. The city's love life is about to explode. In a good way."

The pale blue cup covered with yellow flowers and the word happy mocks my attitude this morning. Everything I was searching for in this career is coming to pass. Why am I not happier about it? I remember Grace's words. "I'm hardly a guru. Newbie is more like it. What event?"

"Friday night at the Coach Room. We are contacting the Love Atlanta Style cast from the last two seasons. The party will be open to the public and you and Ned are going to answer dating questions. Plus, we want Ned to do some matchmaking. We're working on that now."

I pour a splash of almond milk into my steaming coffee. "You can throw all this together by Friday?"

"I can and have. Everything's almost arranged. Emails were sent to the cast last night after I secured the venue. These Love Atlanta Style connections are great. Plus, who wouldn't love this publicity. We are contacting the media. They're hot to cover the nightlife in Atlanta. Big stuff happening. Big stuff. I just wish I knew when I hired you that you knew Ned Parks."

A few sips of coffee raises my boldness to another level. "I didn't know him when you hired me. I just met him Friday night."

Silence.

More silence.

"Sonny. Are you there?" I loudly take a sip of coffee hoping to engage a reaction.

"But you know him, right? Because that picture you tweeted last night looked cozy. I'm counting on cozy, Suzanna."

Musky cologne and black rimmed glasses mold into the vision of Ned turning that vision into Nathan. Nathan and cozy go together. Ned? Not so much. But I won't give my boss a heart attack on a beautiful Sunday morning. "I can play cozy. But it's playing, Sonny."

"Suzanna. You're the best. Have a great Sunday, and keep that advice flowing. You're doing a great job. I knew hiring you would benefit us both."

Benefit? Settling on my couch, I curl my feet underneath me. Why does Grace think my advice is over the top?

My hands wrap around the happy cup and I savor the smell of my coffee. Maybe I'm not cutting Ned enough slack. After all, it wasn't his father's card that was declined. The dinner was very pricey. But still, offering to pay seems like such a guy thing to do.

After taking another sip of my coffee, I set my cup on my coffee table and pick up my phone. I open Twitter and see what's going on. Sunday is the only day I have "off." I'm not required to respond to any tweets, but I still like to see what's happening.

And apparently what's happening is Ned and me. I squint, trying to verify the number of retweets I think I'm seeing. As my brain tries to accept the number, a call comes through.

Nathan.

I find myself smiling as I say, "Hello. Good morning." After tapping the button to turn on the speaker, I lay the phone on my thigh and pick up my coffee.

"Good morning. I called to see how dinner with your father went."

A warm sensation flows through me at how gentlemanly Nathan is. I've tried to stay away from men like him in the past. And have succeeded. They're too nice, not prone to drama. Excitement evades them. And me while I was dating them. So I always said, "See you later."

I'm not sure why Nathan is different. Of course, I've only known him a short time. I haven't had time to miss the excitement that doesn't surround him. "Dinner was interesting."

"Interesting? That's an *interesting* way to describe it. Tell me more."

"Sure. How about I tell you all about it at brunch. Can you meet me in an hour?"

Surprised at my own words, I now think I've had too much coffee.

CHAPTER SIX

"SO, YOUR DAD'S card was declined? I'm sorry." Nathan takes a bite of his eggs, his gaze holding an air of concern.

"It was quite awkward, I must admit." I push the food around on my plate, feeling guilty that almost thirty dollars is going to waste because I'm suddenly not hungry at all.

"Please don't tell me Ned complained about paying the bill."

I chuckle. "No, he didn't complain."

"Good. I guess he is growing up a little."

"He didn't pay the bill."

Nathan's fork stops midway to his mouth. "He didn't pay? So your dad had another card that worked?"

I shook my head. "Oh, no. That would have been convenient. No, I paid. My card was accepted."

Nathan closes his eyes momentarily, like he's thinking, then continues eating. "I would like to say I'm surprised. But I'm probably not."

"He must not give his clients dating advice. Not sure he would be successful in that area. But in all fairness, we weren't on a date." For some reason I want to make that perfectly clear to Nathan.

"Date or not, it would have been the manly thing to do."

Ah. My earlier thoughts run through my mind. Except I used the word guy instead of manly. I like manly better. Especially coming from Nathan. "Well, it's over now. My dad will probably give me the cash when I see him next."

"So you and your dad had a good visit?"

I shrug. "Sure. We never go too deep if you know what I mean. We rocked the usual superficial conversation that doesn't reveal anything about us."

"Even if it's superficial, treasure it. You never know when it may end."

Without thinking, I reach out and grab his hand. "Thank you for reminding me. I guess even the shallow stuff can be missed if that's all you have to miss."

He slips his hand from under mine and places it over mine. "You're different. In a good way."

Warmth from his hand makes me feel safe. Secure. I quickly pull my hand from his. Safety and security are the last things I'm looking for. Because they don't work long-term.

Fun, crazy, and spontaneous. That's the way to go.

Ned. He's all those things.

I dab my mouth with my napkin to hide my confusion. I need some fresh air, a nice walk, and a pedicure. That way I can clear my head. But I can't seem to clear my head with Nathan around.

He only complicates things.

A lot.

And I don't understand why. He's everything I don't want in a guy. So this should be simple. Before I can stand, my phone buzzes. "It's my mom."

As I say hello to Mom, Nathan stays seated. I lose track of what Mom is saying as I notice Nathan's crisp, business look. It's Sunday morning. What happened to wrinkled shirts and a pair of jeans that you might have worn Saturday?

Not sure Nathan knows how to be casual.

I need casual.

"Airport?" I think I hear Mom say that word.

"Yes dear. I'm here at the Atlanta airport. I'm taking a taxi to your condo. I should be there in twenty minutes at the most."

"Mom. What are you doing here?" Thoughts of my parents in the same town for any length of time unnerve me. And watching Nathan give the waiter his credit card unnerves me as well. I didn't expect him to pay for my brunch. I wanted to pay for my own brunch.

"I'm surprising my girl. Is that okay?"

Nathan, Ned, Dad, and now Mom? Last week at this time none of these people were players in my life. At least my Atlanta life. Dad and Mom were far away in their lives and I didn't even know Nathan and Ned. This is crazy. "Of course it's okay. I'll see you at my place."

"Don't sound too excited. Is this a bad time, darling?"

I shake my head. "No, Mom. Never. I'm always glad to see you." Meanwhile, Nathan is signing the bill and I'm trying not to hyperventilate.

"Me, too. See you soon."

Shoving my phone in my purse, I look at Nathan. "Talk about bad timing. My mom is here. In Atlanta. Surprise visit. She'll be at my place in twenty minutes. This is unreal. And my place is a mess. I gotta go. Now. And you didn't have to pay for my brunch, but thank you."

"I wanted to pay. So you're welcome."

61

We walk out of the restaurant, my mind befuddled with my mom's arrival. "I'm just a couple blocks down. Thank you again."

He smiles and I'm inclined to forget about my mom for a moment. But just a moment. I take a step.

"Suzanna. I want to help."

Nathan's sincere expression works its way into my heart. "Help how?"

He grabs my hand and we start walking toward my place. "You said your place was a mess. Four hands are faster than two."

We walk the two blocks quickly, skirting around slower moving people, as I try to process this man who has offered to help me clean my place. Am I really going to let him help? Reaching the front door of my building I stop. "Really, Nathan. You don't have to do this."

"I know. Let's go."

I point to his crisp shirt then my finger motions downward to his nice slacks. "Not exactly cleaning clothes."

"We're down to sixteen minutes until your mom's arrival."

I shrug and motion for him to follow me.

The elevator dings as we reach floor seven. "Here we are."

We quickly make our way down the paisley-patterned carpet hallway to my door. "Ready?" I smile at him before turning my key in the lock.

"Ready," he replies.

We step in and my gaze darts around. Not too bad, I guess.

"Where do you want me to start?"

I walk to a closet and pull out a dust mop. "If you don't mind running this over the floors, I'll tackle the bathroom."

At least I don't have a lot of clutter sitting around. Riley helped me do a purge a couple of months ago. We had opened a bottle of wine and after a couple of glasses we started ditching stuff. It was good for my soul she said.

"Next?" Nathan stands in the doorway as I finish wiping the tub down.

"Do you mind wiping down the kitchen counters? I'll change the sheets on the bed. I hope I have a set of clean ones for the pull-out sofa which will be my bed for as long as she stays. Hello, achy back."

"I'm on it."

My gaze lingers much too long on Nathan walking to my kitchen. But oh, his backside is very nice on the eyes. He must have his clothes tailored to fit. I shake my head, shove the cleaning supplies underneath the sink and head toward my bedroom.

I quickly change the sheets, tossing the dirty ones into the clothes basket in my closet.

Nathan is arranging the couch cushions into place as I enter the living room.

"Found an extra set and made up the couch bed for you."

"Thanks. Really, thanks. I appreciate all of your help."

A knock sounds on the door.

"And not a moment too soon." I take the few steps and look out the peep hole. I always look before opening. But I don't open the door. Instead I turn toward Nathan. "It's my dad."

Nathan cocks his head. "Aren't you going to open the door?"

I put my hand on the knob. "This isn't good. Mom will be here any second."

"Don't they get along?"

I shrug. "I don't know. I don't think they fist fight or anything." I smile, probably to keep from crying.

Another knock sounds, this one heartier, louder.

Turning the knob, I open the door. Not only is my dad standing there, he's carrying two suitcases, one in each hand. And he has a briefcase tucked under his arm. "Come on in."

I grab the briefcase and Nathan quickly steps over and takes one of the suitcases.

"Thank you." Dad sets the other suitcase down.

"So you're leaving town? I could have met you somewhere to say goodbye." I wish we were somewhere else. Anywhere else. My heart is beating fast waiting for the soft knock of my mom. I wonder how long it's been since they've seen each other.

As Dad seems to struggle to answer, I notice his face. It's drawn, and his eyes look tired. His usually well-kept eyebrows look bushy and long, very unlike Jameson Worth. I continue the perusal of my father, something I was obviously too distracted to do last night—his suit looks a bit wrinkled, his shoes aren't shining.

Something is not right.

"I'm not leaving. I actually need a place to stay."

CHAPTER SEVEN

"WHY? WHAT'S GOING on?" Talk about hearts beating fast. My hands are clammy, my knees are shaky. This is not who I am at all.

"I thought you said Ned wasn't your boyfriend. What's he doing here on a Sunday morning?" Dad nods toward Nathan.

"This isn't Ned. It's his twin brother Nathan. And it's not Sunday morning. It's well after noon. You are trying to get out of answering my question. What's going on?"

"Twins? I wondered at the glasses. Nice to meet you, Nathan. Jameson Worth."

Nathan takes Dad's offered hand, and they shake. Dad is drawing this out and Mom will be knocking any second. "Please answer me. Tell me why you need a place to stay."

Nathan moves closer to me. Dad closes his tired eyes for a moment. When he opens them, he opens his mouth like he's about to speak, but before he can utter a sound his mouth shuts at the knock on the door.

Mom.

The term "my nerves are shot" comes to life as I open the door. "Mom."

We hug, her scent familiar and comforting. We end our embrace and I prepare. "Here, let me." I pull her pink suitcase in, and she follows.

Emma Worth only takes a couple of steps in, but she makes an entrance. She's tall, but not as tall as Dad. Her blonde hair, cut short in the back with long, wispy bangs in the front make her look younger than she is. Stylish clothes with matching shoes and handbag tell me Mom hasn't changed one bit. Except maybe her demeanor. She's not her usually smiling self. She looks at me, her eyes slightly narrowed. "What's going on, Suzanna."

I shake my head. "I don't know, Mom. That's what I've been trying to find out. You remember Dad." I laugh like I've made a funny joke. "And this is my friend, Nathan. Nathan, my mom, Emma Worth."

Nathan and my mom shake hands. Dad's eyes spark to life momentarily before returning to their former sad-looking state.

"Suzanna, you know I've always loved your condo, but it's a bit small for four adults, three pieces of luggage and a brief case. So who's leaving? Because if it's me, I'd like to call that nice cab driver that brought me here. He was a gem." Mom focuses on me, probably to keep from looking at Dad.

"I'm sure it's me who's leaving." Dad picks up his briefcase.

I'm confused and not sure what to do. Dad obviously came here with his bags packed for a reason. Where is he going to go?

"My car is just a couple of blocks away." Nathan smiles that smile I'm becoming used to. "Why don't I give you a lift?"

I wish I could say Dad looks relieved, but he almost looks more pained.

"Sure. I'd like that. Suzanna, I'll be in touch." He gives me a kiss on the cheek before grabbing one of his suitcases. "Emma, you are looking well. It's good to see you."

Mom moves out of the doorway. She drops her purse on the couch. "Jameson, your compliments quit impressing me years ago. But I will say it's nice to see you."

"I'll call you later," Nathan says to me as he grabs Dad's other suitcase. I don't even have time to respond before they are both gone and the door is shut.

"Suzanna, darling, what was that about? And who is Nathan? I never thought I'd see you date someone with glasses. Big glasses at that."

"I'm not dating Nathan. He's a friend. And I have no clue as to what is going on with Dad. He came into town yesterday, and we had dinner. But then he showed up here right before you did. Unexpectedly I might add. And what's with your surprise visit?"

"Is Nathan, you know. . ." Mom tries to sport a sly look but fails.

"No. Nathan is not gay. Why would you think that?"

She unwraps her peach-colored lightweight scarf from around her neck. "It's hard for me to imagine a nice young man just being your friend. Unless, of course, he doesn't like women. You are everything a man could want."

I drag my mom's suitcase into my room so she doesn't see the eye roll. According to Emma Worth if you're almost thirty and don't have a man something is wrong with you. Unless you are her daughter, then of course, something is wrong with all the men in the world.

Spotting a pair of sandals sitting almost under the bed, I shove them in the closet before heading to the living room.

"How many years has it been since you and Dad have been in the same room together?"

Mom has taken up residence by my big window. I don't have a view of anything except the apartment building next to me. But the window does let in light. I head into the kitchen, grab a glass and drop a couple of ice cubes into it.

"I'm not sure. Many, many years. He's looking good. Troubled, but good. I wonder what his trouble is now."

I hand Mom a glass of sparkling water. At least I have her favorite drink on hand. "You think he's in trouble?"

"I don't think, I know."

"How can you know? You just said you haven't seen him in years."

Mom swirls the ice around in her glass. "A woman knows when a man is in trouble. Trust me on this."

The thought of Dad in trouble troubles me. The declined credit card pops into my mind. I'll have to text Nathan and see where he took Dad. If he's in a no-tell motel, he might be in a financial bind after all.

But that is hard to imagine. He's been loaded for so long. World traveled and refined. I never quite fit in his schedule. But he's still my father.

I'll focus on Dad later, when Mom isn't around. Time to figure her out. "So, Mom. What's up with this surprise visit?"

She sips her water slowly, a faint smile on her face. "I can't come and see my one and only girl without an agenda?"

I nod. "Of course you can. But you never have." My fingernail taps my glass.

"Oh, all right. I do have an agenda. But you aren't going to like it."

"Of course I'm not. What is it?"

"I want you to move to California. To be near me. There. Is that so bad?"

Panic is the first emotion that hits. "Mom. Are you okay? Are you sick?"

Her amused expression squashes my panic.

"Yes, I'm okay, and no, I'm not sick."

I let my breathing slow along with my heart rate. "Okay. Good. Then why do you want me to move to California? I love Atlanta."

"I know you do, darling. Really, I do. But I'm lonely on the west coast all by myself. I want to have lunch with you. Cook you dinner. Girl things."

My heart rate speeds up again at these admissions from her. "You have amazing friends where you live. And you've never cooked dinner in your life."

Her fingers gently caress her throat, which mean she's thinking. In a moment they'll connect with her necklace and she'll make sure the clasp is at the back of her neck.

"You know what I meant about dinner. Carol still helps out. She's a fabulous cook. Or the club dinners are always well prepared. And nutritious."

I would go and give Mom a hug, but we aren't like that. I think back at Nathan and Ned's family picnic at the winery. Hugs abounded. All families are different, though. What's good for one may not be good for another. But what could be bad about a hug? "Don't you still play bridge a couple of times a week?"

"I do. But we're on hiatus for a couple of weeks. Tannery died, and we have to find a replacement. There aren't as many qualified bridge players as there used to be."

Tannery died? She'd been my mom's best friend for years. This is hug material. "Mom, I'm so sorry," I say as I carefully wrap my arms around her for a second or two, both of us keeping our glasses of the sparkling, bubbly water at arm's length. "Why didn't you tell me? I know this must be devastating."

"Quite shocking, actually. She was fine one day, gone the next. Her heart, they said."

"I'm really sorry, Mom."

"Oh, doll, it's a part of life. But with Bridget, Tonya, and Sal's passing all in the last few months, Tannery's just seems like too much to handle. On my own, that is. The funeral was yesterday, and I just had to get out of there for a few days. Had to."

I wonder how much Mom is thinking of her own mortality in the midst of her friends demises? My mom was thirty-eight when she had me. She and Dad had long given up that kids would happen. Then, the joy of having me was too much, and they divorced when I was two. Dad's business took off and so did he. Mom and I stayed here in Atlanta, but when I moved out, she moved to California where Tannery lived. They stayed single, had fun, and grew old together.

Now Tannery was gone.

Tears threaten as I remember all the crazy times Mom talked about having with Tannery, who'd never married but was loved by many. According to Mom, she broke as many hearts on the west coast as she did on the east coast. She was beautiful, free spirited, and smart.

A part of me feels my mom wanted to be like Tannery. And maybe these last few years Mom had lived the Tannery lifestyle. Now, with Tannery gone, my mom probably is lost.

I think about Grace and Riley. I love them. If something were to happen to either one of them, I know I'd be lost. "I'm glad you came, Mom. Really. We'll have a fun few days. I have a new job now. I work from home. From my phone if I want to."

"That's great, doll. What do you do?"

"Give dating advice to the singles of Atlanta?" I hedge my answer not sure what she will think.

"Are you telling me what you do or are you asking me?"

"Asking for your approval, I guess."

"Honey, you can give dating advice to anyone you want. But don't try giving it to me."

I quickly shake my head. "No way. I would never give advice to you."

"How is it that you can work from your phone?"

We spend the next few minutes scrolling through my Twitter account. I set her up a Twitter account on her phone and push follow on my handle. "There. You are now following me. You can watch me do my job."

"I still can't believe you have more than ten thousand followers on your dating account. Are there that many people desperate for love? Really?"

I try not to take offense to her question. "Desperate? Mom, they're not desperate. Just looking for advice. Geez. I'm not the "you'll never find love unless you take my advice" girl. This is all in fun."

"Some of those people are serious. You know this, right?"

"Yes. But serious is different than desperate."

It's going to be a long few days.

MOM WANTED TO take a quick shower and freshen up, so I decide to run to the grocery down the street to grab a few things. Maybe a couple of chicken breasts for dinner, some veggies and a few things for breakfast. I never buy too much because I go on foot and have to walk with the bags two blocks.

As I exit my building, shopping bags and my purse looped over my shoulder, I call Nathan. It goes to voice mail, so I leave a message for him to call me when he can.

Before I can drop my phone in my purse, I hear someone calling my name.

I turn to find Nathan sprinting toward me. Stepping toward the building front, out of the way of people walking, I stop.

"Hi." He's barely out of breath when he reaches me. "Glad I caught you."

"Is Dad okay? Where did you take him?" Please don't say a cheap motel. Please.

"My place."

"Okay. Is that until a room is ready? I mean, most hotels let you check in at three. It's already almost four."

The street sounds of the city become lost as I watch Nathan. Granted, I don't know him that well, but I know when someone is hedging.

And Nathan is hedging.

"Nathan?"

"Bottom line? Your dad doesn't have anywhere to go. He's staying at my place with me."

"For how long?" My throat is so dry, I'm surprised the words came out as strong as they did.

Nathan shrugs. "Not sure. He literally has nowhere to go."

I shake my head, staring at the tall buildings surrounding us. "That's impossible. He has more than one house."

Gently, Nathan rubs my forearm, drawing my attention away from the impersonal buildings. His touch warms more than my arm, his gaze gives me peace. A strange peace, but peace none the less.

"I think you and your dad need to have a talk. Soon."

I glance at my phone, knowing I need to talk to him in person. A phone call or a series of texts isn't going to cut it for the conversation we need to have. "I will. In person."

"Here, let me." Nathan takes the bags off my shoulder.

"You're going to the grocery with me?" I drop my phone into my purse.

"Why not? Let's go."

We carefully merge our way through the people and walk at a steady pace. Not too slow, not too fast. This is the kind of lazy-day Sunday thing couples do. Except Nathan and I aren't a couple.

We enter the grocery, and I rub my arms at the coolness of the air. Barely into May and already the air conditioners are running strong.

"Cart?" Nathan asks?

Where is my mind? "Sure. A small one will do."

"I'll push. You fill." He sets the bags in the cart, careful to push them against the back so they won't be in the way. Is he always this considerate?

The grocery isn't very big, and we navigate through quickly.

"Dinner for Mom?" Nathan asks as I drop a package of chicken breasts into the cart.

"Yes." The cold air chills me even more. "My Dad. Does he have money for food? Tell me you're not feeding him."

"Calm down. I told him I was going out to grab a pizza for us. Me and him, not me and you. Although truth be told, I'd rather be having pizza with you. Not that there's anything wrong with your dad. Geez, I've made a mess out of these words."

Chuckling, I feel some of the tension leave my body. "It's okay. I know what you mean. Totally."

"Good."

"I'll give you some money for the pizza."

"And I'll refuse it. No need. I can certainly share a pizza with your father and pay for it. What are you going to do with that chicken?"

"Not sure. Bake it I guess. Keeping it simple as I'm not the best cook." That statement alone proves I'm not interested in Nathan. No good southern girl tells a guy she wants to date that she can't cook.

"Can you boil pasta?"

I laugh. "Is that a joke?"

"No. If you can boil pasta, I'll show you how to make a mean fettuccine before I head back to my place."

At my silence, he runs back to a couple of aisles that we've already been down. When he returns, he drops a couple of items in the buggy. "All set."

"Thanks."

We continue moving down the meat aisle. "I'll talk with Dad tomorrow. Thanks for taking care of him tonight."

"Sure. I'm glad to."

We finish shopping, and Nathan carries the bags to my building. "Thank you."

"I'll come up and start the fettuccini, then order the pizza. It should be ready when I get there."

Unlocking the main door, I hold it open so Nathan can walk in. "Dad probably thinks you got lost."

"Doubt it. He was going to lay down. I'm sure he doesn't even know I'm gone."

We ride the elevator up then walk down the carpeted hallway to my door. As I put my key to the lock, I realize the door is ajar. Turning, I look at Nathan and nod toward the door. "It's open." I mouth the words.

Nathan sets the bags down and motions for me to step aside. He pushes the door slightly and takes a tentative step inside. From the profile view I have of him, I see his eyes close momentarily, his long lashes brushing his cheek. He turns, smiling at me before picking up the bags. "Guess who's coming for dinner?"

CHAPTER EIGHT

AN HOUR LATER Mom, Dad, Nathan and I are squeezed around the small table in my condo eating chicken fettuccine, salad and bread. Our plates are touching, and our drinks are clustered in the center of the table. I'm not sure what kind of a conversation Mom and Dad were having before Nathan and I returned, but they haven't had much of one in our presence. To say this dinner is awkward is a true statement.

I want to delve into Dad's issues but not in front of Mom. He took a cab here, so he has to have some money. When asked why he came back here, he said he wanted to talk to me. He said we would talk later, which means we aren't talking in front of Mom.

Although, he knew Mom was here.

There's more to his story. I know it. Mom probably knows it.

Nathan? He catches on quick. I'm sure he knows it.

But for now, we'll play pretty and pretend eating dinner with both of my parents is a normal, everyday occurrence.

"You're quite the cook, Suzanna. This is delicious." Mom takes another dainty bite of her pasta after she speaks.

"Nathan made this. I did put together the salad, though."

"The salad is great." Dad taps me on the forearm like I need his reassurance. Seriously, I don't think I've had this much parenting in my whole life. Why now? I've managed just fine without it so far.

Or have I?

It's weird seeing my dad's big frame cramped into my small dining area. He can't be comfortable. Sitting this close to him, with my condo lighting, I'm noticing creases where I didn't notice them before. His face looks tired and his eyes look lost. Even though my dad and I don't know each other well, it still makes my heart sad to see him like this.

Broken.

I always imagined him out conquering the world. And I'm sure he still can, but whatever has happened has taken a toll.

Our food is a good excuse to keep us from conversing. When Nathan offers to help clean up, I let him. I have no qualms about a man in a kitchen. In fact, I love a man in the kitchen. It doesn't take long to load the dishwasher and wipe down the table. Back in the living room, we find Dad sitting alone on the couch watching the television with no sound.

"Where's Mom?"

He nods toward my bedroom. "She said she needed to rest. She needed a rest from me, I'm sure."

Nathan takes a seat on the end of the couch, and I check out my bedroom. Sure enough she is lying on my bed, her flower-patterned shirt mingling with my flower-patterned comforter.

"You okay?"

She doesn't speak but waves her hand.

Fine.

I go back into the living room then sit between Nathan and my dad. As I settle in, I kind of want to go back to my room and lie down with my mom. It's safe in there. No hard questions to ask. No awkward answers to hear.

"So, Dad. What's going on?" I do keep my voice low, not a whisper, but not overly loud, either.

As he stares down at his hands, he steeples his fingers together. I'm by nature impatient, but I calm myself, giving him time.

When he does look at me, I wished he hadn't. Sorrow fills his expression and my heart. "I've lost it all, Suzanna. Everything."

Nathan stands. "I'll let you guys talk. Just call me and I'll come back for Jameson."

Dad motions for Nathan to sit down. "Nonsense. You've opened your home to me. I've got nothing to hide from you."

Nathan does as Dad wants, but when he sits, he lands much closer to me than he was before. I find it comforting.

"When you say everything, what do you mean? You have more than one house, more than one business."

He nods. "And it's all gone. I'm mortgaged to the hilt on all the homes, my businesses have been failing, and I've been borrowing from one to save another and now it's all come to a head. My houses are in foreclosure and frankly, I'm as drained as my bank accounts. There's nothing left."

"Wow. Just wow. I'm not sure what to say."

"What kind of business did you have?" Nathan asks.

"I owned a construction company. When the crash hit, I thought I scaled back, I was forced to scale back. But then things started looking good again and I over extended. Unintentionally of course, but certain areas didn't grow as fast as others. I was going to save jobs and build houses. Instead I created too much debt and let everyone down."

Dusk falls along with his words, and the room darkens slightly. I leave my place on the couch and turn on the lamps that sit on the end tables. "Do you have a plan?"

"No. No, I don't. I know I need one, but I haven't had the brain power to think."

"Why don't you take a break from all of it for a couple of days?" Nathan stands. "We'll go back to my place and you can rest. We'll reevaluate things Tuesday or Wednesday. How does that sound?"

"I just want to make things right."

"After a couple of days of rest, we'll talk about how you can go about doing just that."

I hug Dad and Nathan as they prepare to leave. I mouth the words "thank you" to Nathan. He smiles and nods. "Glad I can help," he whispers back.

The door isn't shut three seconds before Mom is standing in the living room. "The mighty Jameson Worth has fallen."

85

"And that makes you happy?" The need to know where Mom stands on this is strong.

"No. It may not have worked out for us, but that doesn't mean I want to see him fail."

"What did you two talk about while you were here alone?"

Is that a pink blush developing on her cheeks?

"Nothing of importance. I told him about Tannery." Mom makes her way to the couch. "I told him about how I want you to move to California."

I'm not going to fuel that topic with a response. I love Atlanta and I'm not moving. "How well did Dad know Tannery? You know, back in the day."

"So so. He remembered her. Told me he was sorry."

Mom leans back on the couch. The light hits her face revealing a tear running down her cheek. I hug her as best as I can. "I know it hurts. You can cry."

She holds onto me for a moment. But just a moment. "I've cried too many tears this week. Time to get it together."

"Grief is a process. I don't think there's a time frame on it. She was your best friend."

"She was wise and funny, the perfect compliment to my ditzy, dry-humor self."

Smiling, I grab her hand. "You can stay as long as you'd like." Words I'm sure I'll regret tomorrow.

MOM HAS BEEN in bed for a couple of hours. The pullout couch is worse than I remember.

I finally quit fighting my insomnia and sit up. I grab my phone. My Twitter account has been quiet today. I'm good with that on a Sunday, but I need to ramp this thing up come tomorrow. There has been some activity, though.

Oh. And Ned is chiming in. Great.

I guess it's great. Why do I feel like he's invading my space?

Probably because he is.

But he's so cool. I'm supposed to love him invading my space.

A particular tweet catches my eye. A buildinglife handle tweeted to me, *I'm in love with a girl, but I don't have a job. Should I pursue her or wait until I'm employed?*

I suck my breath in at Ned's reply. *Dude, jobs are good, but love is better. #findworkwhenyoucan #shelovesyouforyou*

Wow. Ned is a romantic. I feel a piece of my heart slip into his words. So he's good looking and a softie for love. It might be nice working with him. I reply to buildinglife, *Find a gal that loves picnics and walks in the park.* *#goodplacetostart*

Feeling warm and cozy, I start scrolling through Twitter. A notification pops up.

buildinglife *I've just moved to the city. Will find parks. Thanks. #simplelife*

Smiling, I reply.

buildinglife—So many great parks around." *#centennialpark* *#fountains #ferriswheel*

After a moment he replies. *Sounds like fun. Any other suggestions in case she says yes to a second date? #realbroke #lookingforajobIpromise*

Now I'm laughing.

I respond. *buildinglife—Window shopping is a girl's best friend."* *#cantgowrong* *#dontoffertobuyanything* *#womenlovemenwhoshop*

There is no immediate reply, and I wonder at this advice. It's all true. I wouldn't steer a man in the wrong direction.

Others are tweeting, but it seems buildinglife and Ned have gone. I answer a gal who wants to know how much time it takes to fall in love.

Really?

I can't hashtag the word really. That would be sarcastic. This is why I don't work before I have coffee. Coffee gives me discernment. And sanity.

I answer that it could take from one second to one decade or longer. Everyone is different. I'm not sure how she will like that response, but it's the truth. There are always the advocates for love at first sight, something I'm not a believer in, but I have to be open to all sorts of scenarios with this job. I will not tell her that after being on Love Atlanta Style, Grace and I determined you can't find love in six weeks. But then Grace went and found it in a couple of weeks, so there went that theory.

I remember the party Sonny is planning for Friday. This morning that was my biggest worry in life.

My, how things can change in a day.

CHAPTER NINE

AFTER LEAVING MY mom with coffee, breakfast, and the promise that I wouldn't be gone long, I head to the office to meet Sonny. I am somewhat surprised to find Ned there as well.

Sonny is on the phone. He nods and motions for me to sit in the chair next to Ned.

Ned who looks up briefly from his phone.

I slide into the chair keeping my gaze on Ned. His sandy-colored hair hangs sexily. When he lifts his head it will fall into place without him doing a thing. Stylish jeans and a trendy-looking button up make him look like the cosmopolitan man of the hour. Comfortable and relaxed. Those are words that describe Ned.

Words I can hang with.

After Sonny places his phone on his desk he turns his attention to Ned and me. "Wow. You two look great together. This is genius. I'm genius. And I have great news for you. Great news."

Both Ned and I stare at Sonny, waiting for this amazing news. I guess Sonny is waiting on a verbal request from one of us. So I succumb. "What is this great news?"

"I thought you'd never ask. I've arranged a television spot for you."

I look at Ned who is now smiling and giving his full attention to Sonny.

"TV?" Ned can't hide the excitement from his voice.

I, on the other hand, feel my insides nervously start to grumble.

"Yes. Two minutes every day Monday through Friday on the Atlanta Unleashed show."

"AU? With the beautiful babe Brittany Benson?" Ned oozes.

He certainly didn't forget Brittany's name. And he sounds so scripted already. He probably practices at this stuff.

"The one and only Brittany. She's looking forward to you two being on the show sharing dating tips. I told her you two had chemistry, great banter together. So don't let me down. Suzanna, your agent will have the paperwork soon. We're dropping the blog thing for now. No-agent Ned, you need an agent. Talk to Suzanna. She has a good one. You both will be paid, of course. And it's all live, so you have to be at the studio everyday at nine for makeup and hair. You'll go on at ten-ten."

"Is this an offer or a done deal?"

Sonny's face scrunches. "Suzanna. You're killing me. You know I'm looking out for you."

"I know you offered me a job hosting a Twitter account. Then you tell me I have to be at an event Friday night. Now you're telling me I have to do a television spot."

Ned brushes my bicep with his fingertips. "Hey. This is a great opportunity. People don't get exposure like this every day."

"Of course you want exposure. You have a business to promote. I'm the Twitter girl. There may be a reason I'm the Twitter girl. Behind the scenes is a very comfortable place to hang." I haven't even told my friends about my job. Now I'm going to be on television? Talking dating advice?

Sonny taps his fingertips on the desk. "Suzanna, why are you balking? This is a two-person gig. No Suzanna, no Ned. And vice versa. It's the two of you or neither of you. We're going to announce this at the party Friday night." Sonny winks at Ned. "Brittany Benson is hosting the party. It doesn't get much better than that, does it?" His gaze now bounces between Ned and me.

"Excellent." Ned nudges me. "This is so cool, isn't it, Susan?"

"Suzanna." I say my name simply, without snark or attitude.

"Right. Not sure why I can't remember that. It's a cool name, though. Really." Ned stares at me as he speaks and can almost believe him.

Almost.

And if he says the word cool one more time I'm going to cool him.

Looking at Sonny, I try keeping previously mentioned snark and attitude out of my voice. "How are we going to do a live two-minute television spot if Ned can't remember my name?"

"Suzanna, Suzanna, Suzanna. I have it. On spot. On it. I'm good. Promise. No mix-ups ever again."

Sonny leans back in his chair. "There you go. Problem solved."

I look between these two men, both of who want me to say yes. If I'm honest, the idea intrigues me. And I'm not a stranger to television. I was on Love Atlanta Style for five weeks before I was sent home by Cole. We did a lot of filming. Two minutes should be a breeze. But daily hair and makeup for a two-minute spot equals insane. At least I'll be paid for getting dolled up every day. That might be a perk.

This might not be a bad gig. I could head to the gym or run every morning. I could shower then head to the studio and let them do my hair and makeup. Professionally. Then two minutes on air and I'm ready to tackle the day. If I were to meet friends for lunch I would look awesome without much effort on my part.

"All right. We'll try it."

"Yes!" Ned lifts his hand to give me a high five, but I leave him hanging.

And I don't even feel bad about it.

I ARRIVE AT my condo to find my mother's nose buried in a book. I never knew her to be a reader, so this surprises me. But as she sets the book on the end table, I notice it doesn't look like a regular book. No, it looks more like a diary or a journal.

That's even more interesting.

"Hi, Mom. I didn't mean to interrupt." I nod toward the end table.

"You weren't interrupting, dear. How did your meeting go with your new boss?"

I toss my purse on the end of the couch and sit next to Mom. "Okay. I'm going to be on a television show."

"Again?" Her look indicates she doesn't approve.

"Just for a couple of minutes a day. Giving dating tips."

She purses her lips and closes her eyes for a moment like she's trying to decide if this is a better or worse gig than being on a reality dating show. "That sounds interesting. But you don't have a boyfriend."

"So? What does that have to do with anything?"

"Don't people want dating advice, tips from someone who is successfully dating someone?"

I roll my eyes. "Mom. No one needs to know about my personal life. They aren't interested in me. They are interested in what I have to tell them so they can be successful in dating. It's all about them."

"If you say so."

My gaze drifts to the book or journal my mom had laid on the table. Now that I'm closer I can see the cover is worn, like the book has been read often. And there is no title. "What are you reading?" I nod toward the table.

Mom looks confused for a couple of seconds, then recovers. "Oh. That's Tannery's. She left it for me. It's a journal."

Now all sorts of crazy warmth and awkwardness fill the space. "Tannery left you her journal? Or a journal for you to use."

"It's hers. It's one of many, but I didn't want to bring them all and weigh down my suitcase. She loved journaling and saw it as a type of therapy." She reaches over and picks up the light blue book.

"I can see that. So did Tannery have any deep, dark secrets?"

"None so far. Just thoughts. And poems. She loved to write poems."

"That's awesome."

As Mom sets the book back on the end table, I notice a tear on her cheek. "Mom, I'm sorry she's gone. I know this must be hard for you."

She brushes the tear away like it's a sign of weakness. "Life happens. We lose people we love all the time."

"There's no shame in grieving. Tannery would be mad if you didn't shed a couple of tears, right?"

Mom laughs. "She would want full-on drama tears. With hiccups and everything."

"True. She would. But that's not you."

"No. Tannery and I were very different. But I loved her. She was a true best friend. Do you have a true best friend, Suzanna?"

Wow. Talk about catching me off guard. "Good question. I have a few really good friends. And I guess there are a couple of girls I call when something happens. So yes, I think I do."

"Work on it. When you can say I know I do, then come and tell me. Find that girl, Suzanna. The one you'll trust with your life."

I haven't even told any of my friends about my job. I've only told Ned and Nathan. People I didn't even know this time last week.

Maybe I do need to work on cultivating good friendships.

Amazing friendships.

Friendships that will last a lifetime.

CHAPTER TEN

I STARE AT my phone after leaving messages for Grace and Riley. I refuse to feel paranoid about not having a good friend. They are my good friends; they're just busy at work now. I'm sure that's it. That's the reason neither answered my call.

Before I become too deep into self-pity my intercom buzzes.

Wondering if it is my dad, I push the talk button. "Hello."

"Suzanna. It's Nathan. Can I come up?"

"Sure." I push the button that allows the door downstairs to open while wishing my heart would stop beating so fast. Nathan is here. While seeing Ned this morning has drifted far out of my thoughts, Nathan has never been out of my mind for long.

And now he's here.

As soon as he knocks, I open the door, refusing to acknowledge that it might look desperate. My breath does hitch, but Nathan isn't the only reason.

My father is standing behind him.

And I feel terribly foolish.

My father sucked Nathan into coming over.

When did my father start needing a buffer? Is he afraid of me now that he's admitted he's broke?

Thank goodness for autopilot, because that's where I'm operating from. Add embarrassment to stupid and you have autopilot. "Come on in."

Nathan smiles, and I swear I see a bit of apology in his smile. Like he knows he's been played. And he knows that I know as well.

And add to that I feel my mom's eyes boring through the back of my head. Don't think that feeling goes away after you grow up.

It still happens.

And the older you are the harder the eyes bore.

"Hello, Nathan, Jameson. Suzanna didn't tell me you were coming over."

"Suzanna didn't know. We just kind of crashed."

I love Nathan's tone. Like this isn't a big deal.

"Oh, okay." Mom takes a seat on the couch.

"Actually, I have to borrow Suzanna for a couple of hours. So I brought Jameson to keep you company while I steal her away. Is that okay?"

I search Nathan's eyes for some explanation. Like they might say something his words aren't saying. "Why do you need to borrow me? I'm not something you check out, like at the library."

"I'll explain on the way. Ready?"

"Ready for what? I have no idea where we are going, if I'm dressed appropriately."

Nathan's look makes me want to follow him anywhere. "You look perfect."

And with those words I grab my purse and wave to Mom. "I'll be back." I pick up the remote and hand it to my dad. "Find something you both want to watch. If that's possible. I'm sure we won't be gone long, right?"

After he takes the remote, I look at Nathan.

"Not too long. Promise."

Mom's eyes say she wants to object, but she doesn't. She does move from the couch to the chair next to the couch. I'm sure she doesn't want to take a chance that Dad would sit close to her.

Nathan and I ride the elevator in silence, like if we speak somehow my parents will hear us. The minute we step out of the main doors on to the street, I turn to him. "Okay. So what's up? Where are we going?"

My body is kind of zigging and zagging simply at being around Nathan. Although he does seem somewhat nervous.

We keep walking side by side, me distracted and curious. Nathan quiet for a moment.

"I don't know."

"What do you mean you don't know?"

"I'm doing your dad a favor."

Now I stop and turn to him. "What kind of favor?"

People stop and give us odd looks at having to go around us. Muttering under breath is heard, probably bad words.

"He's a very persuasive man, your dad." Nathan pushes the bridge of his glasses.

"Persuasive how? What is this about?"

"I think he's trying to win your mom back."

I wipe the back of my hand across my forehead. "Okay. We're going back. This is ridiculous. Mom is furious, I'm sure."

He places his hand on my forearm. "Wait. Let's talk about this." He gently takes my hand, and we start walking away from my building.

My mind is whirling from the combination of his touch and his words. He hasn't let go of my hand, and I don't initiate it, either. We slip into a small restaurant and he asks for a table for two.

Two. Me and Nathan.

Not Ned.

Nathan and I aren't meant to be together. He's too regimented. We don't see life the same way. I love nightlife, he doesn't. But he's gentle and kind and helping my dad win back my mom.

I let go of his hand, partly because I don't want to keep feeling his touch and partly because I have a little attitude regarding his helping my father.

We are seated in a corner. Low lighting, white table cloth, candles, and a single rose scream intimacy. I sit up straight, not wanting to acquiesce to the atmosphere. To Nathan.

"Would you like a glass of wine?" Nathan is scanning the wine list.

"I guess."

"Don't sound so thrilled."

"I have questions."

The waitress takes our wine orders. "Are you hungry? I'd love to buy you dinner."

"You're trying to make sure I'm not mad."

"I'm not nearly as diabolical as you think I am."

102

I do half smile at his use of the word diabolical. Nathan could never be diabolical. Ned, now that might be another story. "Look. My mom and dad, together as a couple, isn't going to happen. He left her years ago, and now he's broke. I can't wrap my head around this whole situation with my dad, let alone adding this other craziness with my mom."

"Of course you know your parents better than I do. Your dad is going through a tough time right now. I think your mom might represent some stability for him."

"He should have thought stability when he decided brick and mortar buildings holding his companies were more important than my mom. And me."

Nathan fiddles with the handle of his fork. "I'm not going to argue with you. Not my place. But sometimes people change. Their values and vision changes."

Swallowing hard, I stare at Nathan, trying to make sense of his words in my world.

"It's just something to think about," he says.

"You know my dad has been one big disappointment after another. I don't want him doing that to my mom."

"I can't imagine that. I don't know how you're feeling. But Jameson and I have had a couple of heart to hearts, and I think he's genuine."

103

"Of course you do." Tears form, and I dab the corners of my eyes. "I would give anything to have a heart to heart with my dad."

He takes one of my hands in his, his thumb caressing the tears on my fingers. "I'm a guy. For some guys, it's easier. Plus, he doesn't know me. It's hard to open up to people you love."

Love. What is love? Here I am, supposed to be giving dating advice to the city of Atlanta, and I have no idea what love is. My parents haven't modeled it for me either.

I feel like a fake. A phony.

But the feeling of his hand on mine doesn't feel fake. It feels real. And nice. And something I could become used to.

Gently, I slip my hand away from his. His eyebrows raise, his eyes question, but I don't answer. I simply fold my hands in my lap, knowing they are where they should be.

"I don't know how I let you talk me into this." I say this after he's placed our dinner orders with the waitress. "This is something Ned would do, not you."

Nathan sits straighter. "What is that supposed to mean?"

I sip my wine before answering. "Ned seems to be the wild, spontaneous one. I feel like you think about things more before acting on them."

"What makes you think I didn't think on this?"

I shake my head. "Maybe you did, but knowing my parents this doesn't seem like a good idea at all. But then again, you don't really know my parents."

"I may not know your parents, but I know love."

Now I sit straighter as a chill ripples through my body. "Love? Who is in love?"

His eyes are so serious behind his black-framed glasses. "Your dad. He does love your mom."

Relief or disappointment, I'm not sure which, replaces the chilled feeling. "My dad is not in love with my mom. My dad is apparently desperate and doing what he can to find a home. That's my guess. He has nowhere to go and he needs somewhere to go. He knows he can't stay with me and I guess he's playing on my mom's caring heart."

"There's no cutting slack with you, is there? I think if you had a conversation with him, you would see things differently."

"Maybe so. But having a conversation with my dad that has any depth and meaning hasn't happened in the past, and I don't see it changing now. Last night was the most personal I've talked to Dad ever."

"Your dad is changing. He wants to change. He knows he made mistakes."

The waitress slides our plates in front of us, and I choose this moment to end this conversation. My dad has made mistakes. We all have. But what a convenient time to acknowledge them and want to change.

Jameson Worth may have fooled Nathan, but he's not fooling me.

And he won't be fooling Mom either. She'll see through his fakeness and tell him to go away.

At least I hope she does.

WE ARRIVE BACK at my place to find it empty.

Well, there is a note.

The note says Mom and Dad have gone out and will be back soon.

"Well, what do you know," Nathan says. "Looks like they may be out on a date."

"Ha. Not hardly. Mom probably felt sorry for him and offered to buy him dinner since neither of them can cook."

I drop my purse on the couch then stand next to the window. My condo takes on a different feel with Nathan here. I look outside as if changing my focus will change the feel of my place.

It was different when we were rushing around cleaning.

Never mind that it's dusk outside. My condo already has a low-lit atmosphere, and the fact that I keep thinking about the feel of his thumb as he dried the tears off my hands causes my heart and mind to go places I don't want them to go.

At least he is across the room.

The tiny room. The condo isn't that big.

I still feel his presence.

"I'm sorry if I disappointed you."

His words are close, which means he is close.

Really close.

"You didn't disappoint me. Like you said, my father is persuasive."

I feel him leave me, the space where he stood now empty, and moments later I hear the door click. Now disappointment falls all over me.

He left.

Turning, I'm surprised to see him on this side of the door, his hand on the lock.

Our gazes meet, and I'm drawn into whoever lives behind those beautiful blue eyes. I'm now leaning against the wall next to the window, my heart out of control, my mind frenzied with anticipation.

Because I know Nathan is going to kiss me.

I know it like nothing else I've ever known.

He walks slowly to me. Like we're filming a movie and our goal is to drive the audience crazy. I don't know what to do with my hands because they want to be on him.

In moments they are.

They're around his waist as he places his hands on the wall on either side of me. His head lowers to mine and our lips meet. I've never been kissed like this, because I've never been kissed by Nathan.

My knees weaken and my hands hold tighter to him, a necessity if I want to remain standing. My lips have found their home as he continues to kiss me with abandon. I want more.

I want to be closer.

I loosen the grip I have on his waist, but tighten it once again as his lips leave mine only to find my neck. I moan as his hands dig into my hair and his lips move lower. He pushes my shirt off my shoulder, his kisses covering the place the material has left.

His fingers slide under my bra strap, and it begins.

My undoing.

CHAPTER ELEVEN

I CLOSE MY eyes anticipating the soft touch of his hands, the amazing brush of his fingertips on my skin.

One, two, three seconds go by.

Nothing.

"You're so beautiful." His words caress me, but his hands don't.

As if he's running our film backward, he kisses the top of my shoulder before righting my bra strap. He pulls my shirt in place as he kisses his way up my neck. His lips meet mine again. Soft, gentle.

Captivating.

Claiming.

I'm so confused.

Happy, but confused.

He kisses the tip of my nose then my forehead. He steps back, his hand cupping my face. "I could get into a lot of trouble with you."

My skin is still on fire from his touch. "Trouble never sounded so good."

"You do things to me, Suzanna. Make me act in ways I don't normally act. Think in ways I don't normally think."

He's no longer touching my face. His hands are on his hips as he takes a couple of steps away from me.

"You make it sound like a bad thing. Is it?"

"No. It's not bad, it's different."

I walk to him. "Hold me. Please?"

Our arms wrap around each other like they were made only for this moment. I stare up at him, loving everything that is in my view. "You locked the door. You knew you were going to kiss me. You didn't want my parents walking in. You did that."

He closes his eyes for a second. "I did."

"So you wanted to kiss me."

"Kissing you has consumed my thoughts."

"Then why are we wasting time talking?" I move my arm from his waist and wrap it around his neck, drawing his head down. He hesitates momentarily, but then crashes his lips into mine in a mind-blowing kiss.

We pull apart, breathless. I place my hands on his chest then start unbuttoning his shirt.

"Suzanna," he starts, but I don't let him finish. I place my finger on his lips while my other hand works the remaining buttons. I stop short of untucking his shirt. Instead, I slip my hands inside, my fingertips trembling as they meet his flesh.

I hear him suck in his breath as I run my hands across his tight abs, around his hips to his back, where my fingertips trace a slow path up his spine. His shirt has no choice but to slip away from the confines of his pants.

Staring at his body, I realize I'm gone. Mentally I know nothing but this man in front of me. Physically, I want nothing more than Nathan. All of him.

I look at him. "You're the one who's beautiful."

Our lips meet again gently. Oh, so gently. He's acting like I might break if he presses too hard. My hands roam his chest, abdomen, back.

He shivers, his torso trembling at my touch.

I want to die right now.

No, not now, after.

After this scorching time with this man.

It only takes me seconds to slip off his shirt. "You won't be needing this." I toss it on the couch, only briefly glancing at him. His body perfect.

His body that trembles at my touch.

"And you won't be needing these," I say as I slip off his glasses. And no, I don't toss them on the couch. I take the couple of steps to lay them on his shirt.

I grab his hand.

But as I take a step, he doesn't budge. He lets go of my hand. "Don't tell me you've decided to play hard to get." I laugh, waiting for him to join in.

But he doesn't.

Looking at him I see everything has changed. His gaze searches mine, his lips look cold, and I'm at a loss to what has happened.

I reach out, and he blocks my hands from touching him. "What's wrong, Nathan?"

"At least you got my name right?"

Taking a step back, I cross my arms. "What are you talking about?"

He reaches down, grabs his glasses, and puts them on. "This is who I am, Suzanna. I'm Nathan, not Ned."

"And I'm confused. I know who you are." I'm not sure I've ever had a more gorgeous man standing half naked in my condo. He is body beautiful. But his words aren't making sense at all.

"But you want me to be someone else. I know your sights have always been on Ned, but you've gotten to me.

113

I like you. I thought I could be more than your vehicle to my brother, but I guess I was wrong."

He starts putting on his shirt.

"Men are from Mars has never been more true. I have no idea what you are talking about."

He takes a momentary break from tucking his shirt in and points to his glasses. "These are me. I choose to wear glasses. I like them."

My mind goes back to the first day I met Nathan, and the comment I made regarding his glasses. But he offered to take them off.

For money.

I guess I did tell him I'd pay him to keep them off.

True, my idea of a really hot guy didn't include thick black glasses, but that was then.

Nathan has changed my mind about men with glasses. "I just thought you'd be more comfortable not having to worry about them—"

"No. *You* were going to be more comfortable."

I'm starting to think this goes deeper than the glasses. "For the record, I like you, too. A lot. I'm sorry my taking off your glasses seemed like an insult to you. That wasn't my intent."

He digs in his pocket and hands me a twenty-dollar bill. "Give this to your father for a cab ride to my place. I'll see you later."

With those words he leaves.

Just leaves.

No goodbye, no kiss, no nothing.

All the hotness of the last few minutes simply doused with cold water.

Yes, Atlanta. I'm the gal who gives dating advice.

Tip number one. When undressing your man, don't ever take off his glasses.

NO AMOUNT OF washing my face can erase the feeling of Nathan's lips on mine or the sensation of his hands' gentle caress. I even use cold water and it doesn't help.

Wishing I could crawl in my bed and forget the whole evening, I settle for sitting on the couch in my comfy pajamas, waiting for Mom and Dad. I eye the twenty dollar bill sitting on the end table, and thoughts of Nathan assail me once again.

How did the evening escalate to amazingness only to derail with a simple gesture? I hadn't thought of Ned once, not once, while I was with Nathan tonight. His compassion and kindness have stolen my heart. That's where I was operating from.

Not wishing he was Ned.

No amount of rehashing will change the situation. I'll probably never see him again, unless it has to do with my dad.

Picking up my phone I decide to go to work. Maybe it will keep my mind off my crazy love life, never mind my thoughts about why and where my parents are out together.

I know that's not a date by any means, but it's still strange.

After almost forty-five minutes of giving dating advice I sign off and set my phone on the table.

Next to the twenty dollars.

I pick up Tannery's journal. I don't open it, but I hold it in my hands, the feel of it weighty, heavy, with the promise of more than words.

A journal is different than a diary, right? I'm not sure girls have diaries anymore. Now we have social media where we bear our hearts, our woes, and our joys to the world. We've lost the art of secrecy.

The art of dreaming dreams only we knew.

116

Now the world can lift us up or crush our dreams. A casual phrase here, a well-meaning but demeaning sentence there. We've got so much to influence us now.

Deciding it wouldn't be a breach of girl conduct, I open the journal. After all Mom did say Tannery had written poems. I flip through quickly with an honest attempt at not reading anything. Page after page filled with words. An occasional sketch marked some of the pages. Every now and then a colored ink would replace the standard black. There were hearts doodled on the edges of some of the pages.

I flip through the pages again, slower this time, taking in a word or two. I stop flipping when I see a page titled One Love. This page has an abundance of hearts doodled around the edges.

Of course I can't help myself.

I have to read.

> *Hearts filled with emptiness*
> *Lives that are just a mess.*
> *Broken roads and shattered dreams*
> *Nothing is ever as it seems.*
> *I run, I walk, I try to fly*
> *But I never really reach the sky.*
> *Then comes along my saving grace*

Kissing me gently, cupping my face.
His hands so strong, his heart so sure
For a moment I think he is my cure.
Then darkness falls as he leaves me here
I find I shed just one tear.
Not two, not three, not any more
Than one, for my love walked out the door.

I shut the book quickly, my gaze darting around the room to see if there are any cameras, you know like someone is playing a joke on me.

Than one, for my love walked out the door.

Really?

Not that I consider Nathan my love, but he did kiss me, his hands did cup my face. He did walk out the door.

I don't have time to ponder much more because I hear my parents outside the door. I quickly set the journal on the table as they walk in. I stand, and try to clear my mind so I can have a conversation that makes sense.

But I can't help but think of the poem.

When did she write it? Who did she write it about? Did she write it about anyone in particular or were the words simply words on a page that had no deeper meaning.

"Suzanna, where's Nathan?"

My father's voice cuts through my mind drama. "He had to leave. He asked that you take a cab home." I say the words without emotion, I hope.

I don't want to bring up the subject of money and ask if Dad has enough to take a cab. I'll slip him the twenty when he's on his way out the door.

"It's been a tiring evening. I'm turning in. Good night, Suzanna. I'll see you in the morning."

Mom gives me a barely there hug before disappearing into my bedroom. She shuts the door leaving me and Dad alone.

His expression is one of exasperation. I'm not sure if it's directed toward Mom or the fact that Nathan has left.

Nathan.

Lips. Hands. Body perfect.

Glasses.

I'm still baffled at how things went down. A simple move that changed everything.

"Did Nathan leave anything for me?" Dad asks.

Wow. Life must be bad if he's asking if Nathan left him money. Dread slowly makes its way through my body as I contemplate how broke Dad must be. I hand him the twenty. "Here. He left this."

I couldn't look him in the eye. Jameson Worth has hit rock bottom. And I don't even know him well enough to talk about it.

"This is thoughtful. Unnecessary, but thoughtful. I do have cab money. What I don't have is his address. Did he leave his address?"

He shoves the twenty in his pocket as he speaks.

"No. He didn't."

Dad nods toward the hallway. "I have to go to the bathroom. Can you call or text him for me?"

He doesn't wait for my answer.

Call or text.

Call or text.

Such a dilemma.

I grab my phone and in seconds I hear my phone dialing his number. I know he's going to know it's me. I know the tone of the hello will speak volumes.

"Hello?"

His hello is questioning, not demanding. It has an air of "are you really calling me" that's implied in a good way, not a bad way. It almost says "I was hoping you would call."

"Hi. It's me. Suzanna. Who loves the way your lips feel on mine. Loves the way your fingers feel on my skin.

120

Suzanna, who should have never slipped your glasses off. That Suzanna."

Even through the phone I hear his breath hitch. I can almost see the smile on his face.

"Is that an apology?"

"Doing stupid things unintentionally don't require an apology. Don't you agree?"

"Unintentionally is the key word. I'm more on the deliberate side of the coin."

"I can't wait to change your mind. But for now, my dad needs your address."

"Dad or you?"

"I promise I'm not hijacking the cab ride. Although I don't think you'd protest too much. Would you?"

He doesn't respond right away.

Dad comes back into the living room and mouths the word "thanks" when he sees I'm on the phone.

"Suzanna, we should keep our relationship status as just friends. I see things you don't and frankly I am not my brother in any way, shape, or form. I'm Nathan, a financial planner who isn't enthralled with the nightlife scene."

He then gives me his address.

Repeating the address in my mind I walk to the kitchen where I have a pen and paper. I quickly scrawl the address then tear the paper off the notepad.

Now I am being deliberate at pushing his words of why we can't be together in the back of my mind, refusing to think about them now.

"Thank you, Nathan. He should be there shortly. I do appreciate everything you are doing for him. And I'm not sure I want to be friends."

I end the call without waiting for a response.

Yes, it is a childish move.

But I'm feeling childish right now.

I can't have what I want and it's not fair.

Back in the living room I hand Dad the piece of paper. "Here's his address."

"Thank you. He's a nice guy, Suzanna. Very nice."

I refuse to give my father false hope. "We're just friends, Dad."

He cocks his head. "Say what you want, I see something different."

"Maybe you need glasses then." I speak those words without thinking, my heart diving a little as I do.

"I don't think so." He fiddles with the paper in his hand.

"Where did you and Mom go, and what's going on with that?"

My own misery had let their surprise outing slip from my mind for a while.

"We had eaten sandwiches here and frankly neither one of us wanted to talk about anything important, so we went for a walk. We stopped and looked at the displays in the windows of the shops. Your mom loves clothes. She said she was glad they were closed or she would have spent a fortune. At least she has a fortune to spend, huh?"

"I'm sorry about everything that has happened. Even though I have no idea what happened, I'm still sorry."

"It's okay, Suzanna. I don't want you to worry your pretty self about me or my bad decisions."

"If you ever want to talk I'm here. I've been told I'm a good listener." Okay, so that's not true, but if it will cause him to open up to me, it's okay stretching the truth a little.

"Thanks. And thanks for the pb and j. I haven't had one of them in a long time. Although, the way things look, it might be my go-to sandwich." He laughs.

I don't. "You guys made pb and j's? That was your dinner?"

He had one hand on the door about to walk out. "We did. Reminded me of old times. Good times."

"How does she feel about you trying to win her back?"

He lowers his gaze. When he lifts it I see vulnerability. Then with the swish of the door he is gone.

And for the first time I had a glimpse of the man my mom fell in love with.

Love.

Tannery's poem.

Nathan.

Are things starting to fall into place?

Or are they simply falling apart.

CHAPTER TWELVE

MOM WAS ALL for me going to lunch with Grace and Riley. I asked her to come along, but she said no. She wanted to stay home and eat a pb and j. I didn't say anything to her about what Dad had said last night, but I'm wondering just how much they have in common.

Or maybe just how memories from long ago are sometimes meant to be lived in for longer than a night.

As I walk the few blocks to the restaurant, I think about how Mom looked more settled today. More like herself. I wonder if she talked to Dad more about about Tannery or her wanting me to move to California.

I spot Riley in the restaurant. She's already sitting at a table. I wave and we hug when I reach her. I notice then it's a table for two. "Grace isn't coming?"

She shakes her head as she sits. "No. She got a call that one of the contractors was ready to walk out on the restoration job they have going on. She and Justin had to drive to Lake Hartwell this morning."

"Geez, that's a long way. The perils of owning your own business, huh?" I pick up the menu, promptly deciding on a salad.

"Yeah." She sips her water flavored with lemon and lime. The small bowl littered with the squeezed fruit sits on the table in front of her.

We place our orders with the perky waitress named Rose.

Riley looks pensive. Just like she has the last couple of times I've seen her. Her blondish-brown hair is long and gorgeous as usual, but her eyes have lost their sparkle. The Riley sparkle, I used to call it when we were filming Love Atlanta Style.

"What's going on, Riley? I can tell something is bothering you." Might as well bring it out in the open. Deal with it. Isn't that what friends are for?

"Nothing is going on. How about with you?"

I'm not sure why she's dodging me, but she is. "You look like something is troubling you. Are you sure you're okay?"

She smiles and nods. "I'm perfectly fine. Life is great." She glances at her watch.

"What time do you have to be back?" Riley's job as an executive administrative assistant for one of the

126

leading tech companies in Atlanta is demanding to say the least. The owner of the company, Prescott Wentworth, is hot, single, and oh, so nice. Grace and I keep telling Riley she should pursue him, but she vehemently disagrees.

"One fifteen. We have plenty of time. Anything new with you?"

"Only everything." In the briefest amount of time possible, I tell her about my new job, Mom, Dad, Ned, and Nathan.

Nathan.

Just talking about him brings back memories of our hot kisses from last night.

"Suzanna. I never thought I'd see the day." She smiles coyly at me.

"What day?"

"The day you fell in love. You absolutely light up talking about that man."

My heart twists. I know she's talking about Ned, because I barely mentioned Nathan, the twin brother with the glasses. I didn't tell her about the kisses. I want to keep them all to myself as they probably won't happen again. "I'm not in love with Ned. He's great and everything I could ask for in a guy, but it's not there. Promise."

"I wasn't talking about Ned. I was talking about Nathan."

With great finesse, I wave my hand in front of me. "Nathan? I barely said two words about him. He's a financial planner, remember? Nine to five job. Black glasses. Traditional to the hilt. So not my type. No."

"I wish I had a video of how your eyes and facial expression came to life when you spoke about him. I see it. Maybe you don't, maybe you are in denial, but I see it."

Thankfully Rose decides to set our meals in front of us at this moment. Saves me from an immediate response. I don't think Riley's words deserve any response, really, but to not speak up might be perceived as agreement.

But to deny might be perceived as desperation.

Riley points her fork at me. "Just the way you say his name, like it's caressing the wind, says a lot."

"Have you been reading poetry? Who talks like that? Caressing the wind?" I shove a bite of salad in my mouth.

Saying the word poetry reminds me of Tannery's journal and the crazy poem I read after Nathan left. I shove another bite of salad in, refusing to dwell on the coincidence.

"Hey, I just speak truth. I'm thrilled that you've found someone. Even if you don't know you've found someone. Time will tell on this. Trust me."

"You keep dreaming. Remember, I'm hanging out with Ned Friday night. It's weird, because this guy is who I've been dreaming of my whole life. Seriously, I'm speaking truth here. Maybe it was the circumstances that Ned and I met that has us off kilter. Maybe if we could have alone time it will make more sense. I mean, the only time we've been alone was in his car for about an hour and a half. Either he was on the phone or one of his favorite songs was on the radio. He has a lot of favorites I found out."

Riley gives me a sideways look.

As I continue to eat, I try to convince myself that Ned and I can have a chance. We're both night people. We both thrive on attention. We both love our dating-related jobs.

Really, we're perfect for each other.

Right?

MY JOB IS so much fun! And I am serious.

I'm sitting on my couch, working from my tablet. I'm glad I had a light salad for lunch. Heavy food always makes me sleepy in the afternoon. And I don't have time for sleepy. Not with all these people wanting dating advice.

More and more people are starting to come back for advice as their relationships are progressing. Other people are keeping me apprised of their relationships. This is great. Maybe, just maybe, I'll see a wedding.

Oh, that would be the best! People following dating advice that I give them and actually pledging to love each other for the rest of their lives.

I can hardly breathe thinking about it.

Oh, and here's buildinglife, tweeting to me again. *Things are moving along with my girl. Turns out she likes simple #thanks*

buildinglife—glad to hear it. You know the acronym KISS. Sounds like you found the perfect girl for you. #love #romance #loveat1style

buildinglife answers, *LOL! I'm in agreement all the way.*

I always like to have the last comment, you know just to let them know I saw their last comment. I don't want anyone to ever think I've left them hanging. *buildinglife— sounds like you are building life. Awesome! #justdoit #yourock*

After a minute or so, there's no response. He's probably with his girl now, or planning something fun and cheap for them to do. I wonder why guys always think they need to impress us with expensive things? A few girls have ruined it for the rest of us.

Some of us don't mind a pb and j now and then.

My body flushes at that thought. My dad and his pb and j thing now has my mom on one. Nothing says simple like a pb and j. But Dad isn't doing the pb and j thing because he wants to. He's doing it because he has to.

There is a difference.

And Mom?

She'll go along with anything to keep her too distracted to think about Tannery. I hope it distracts her enough that she forgets about how she asked me to move to California.

"Suzanna, are you still working?"

Mom has been doing her hair and makeup in the bathroom. She hasn't mentioned going anywhere, but then again she knows my limited cooking skills, so she probably assumes we are going out to eat.

"I'm about to sign off. I love it that people I've been giving advice to have relationships that are actually working out." I don't mention the wedding part to her. I know it's dramatic. She wouldn't have the appreciation for the possibilities like I do.

"I'm glad your job is fulfilling, Suzanna. I really am. It's good to see you happy. And it's good to see it's a job that you can do from wherever you are. Like California, maybe."

I close my twitter app and set my tablet on the end table, next to Tannery's journal. "Mom, it would be hard to manage an Atlanta dating scene if I'm not in Atlanta. Right?"

"It's not like you don't know what it's like in Atlanta. If you were on a vacation, you could still work. So why couldn't you work from another state?"

"Mom, vacation is a week or a few days. What if I'm in California and a restaurant I love here in Atlanta closes? Then if I tell someone to take their s/o to it, I look stupid. I have to be here where things are happening."

"What do you mean s.o.?"

"Significant other."

"I see. Well, since you are done working, do you mind taking me to Nathan's? I have something I need to discuss with your father."

Mom's carefully applied makeup and nice outfit take on a new meaning. She can't be interested in Dad again. Can she? "Mom, what's this about?"

"Nothing for you to worry over. If you can't do it, I can take a cab. It's no trouble."

I look down at my workout pants and loose-fitting shirt. I've got light makeup on from meeting with Riley. My hair is pulled into a messy bun. Of course I'm thinking about Nathan. But I'm not going to see him. It's only four o'clock. He's still working. Besides, he wants to be friends only. "No, I'll take you. But let's go so I can get back before traffic gets worse."

It doesn't take us long to arrive at Nathan's building. I'm not sure I like how close he lives to me. Now that I know him, the chances of running into him are quite good. I have to pull into the parking garage because there is an accident in front of his building. Two police cars have the lane blocked.

I grab a ticket and enter the garage, looking for elevators. Moments later, after going up one level I spot them. "Here are the elevators, Mom. They should take you to the lobby, I'm guessing. I assume you and Dad have a plan of where you are meeting, right?"

"Um, yes. I'm supposed to go straight up to the floor the condo is on. Twelve. Do you think I can take these elevators all the way to the twelfth floor?"

The car behind me honks, and I pull into a spot, trying not to be aggravated with Mom. "I don't think so. You'll probably have to get off in the lobby, then take another set to the twelfth floor."

Her expression says confused, but I refuse to believe it. She's a grown woman of high intelligence. She can figure this out.

"Okay. I've got it. I'll take these elevators to the lobby, then find the elevators that will take me to Nathan's floor. Thank you, dear, for driving me. You're a doll. I'm sorry about having to pull into the garage. Do you want some money so you can get out?"

I shake my head. "It's okay. I have my purse and wallet and everything. I can manage."

"Well, the point of you driving me over was to save money on a cab, now you'll have to spend money on getting out of the garage."

My head is about to explode. Who is this woman who used to be my Mom? "No worries. I've only been in here less than five minutes. They may not even charge me."

She opens her door. "I hope they don't, honey. I hope they don't. Have a nice evening. I'll call you when I'm ready to come back. Is that okay?"

"Sure. Just call or text and I'll be at the front. Surely the accident will be cleared by then."

"Love you, honey." With those words she shuts the door, and I sigh. I have no idea what is happening with her.

Before I can fully breathe in from the sigh I breathed out, I see her hand grab the side of my car as she falls.

I jump out of the car and run around to her. She isn't on the ground, but is almost there, both hands on the door handle. I scoop her up and she holds on tight. "Honey. Thank you. I guess I lost my footing. You saved me from severe knee damage, I'm sure."

We're both breathing hard. I hug her. "Are you all right?"

"I am." She breaks our embrace, her hand brushing down her clothes like our hug wrinkled them.

"You're going to be okay?"

She slips her purse back onto her shoulder. "Of course. Don't you worry."

I juggle my keys from hand to hand. "All right."

She starts walking toward the elevator, a definite limp apparent. I lock my car and quickly catch up to her. "Here. Lean on me."

"This is silly. I'll be fine." But her grip on my arm says differently.

She pushes the button for the elevator.

"Mom. How about you skip this visit, and I take you to the doctor. You're really limping."

Shaking her head, she rolls her eyes. "Nonsense. This will work itself out by the time I get to the lobby. I'm not going to the doctor."

A thin layer of sweat shines on her forehead despite the breeze blowing through the parking garage. I think she's hurting more than she wants to admit.

Why is she so stubborn?

The elevator dings, and we step in despite her protests that she doesn't need me going with her. Never mind I'm not dressed to go out anywhere. I know a lot of gals run around in their workout clothes, but I'm not one of them.

Normally.

But these last few days have been nothing like normal.

We step into a grand lobby.

Nathan must do well as a financial planner.

I don't let my mind shift to him, instead I focus on Mom. She takes a couple of steps, and her limp is no better. "I'm thinking doctor."

"I'm not."

Her tight grip holds onto my arm as we enter the elevator. She pushes the button, and we're on our way to Nathan's condo.

I'm not nervous that I might see him. I'm nervous that I'm going to get a glimpse of who he is by what his place looks like. Although I'm not staying long. Just dropping Mom off with Dad.

I can't even say how crazy it all is.

"Are you sure you don't want me to take you to the doctor? You aren't putting weight on your foot at all." We are now walking down the hall.

Slowly.

"Nonsense. I'm putting more weight on it each step. See?"

She falters somewhat at her brave attempt.

I shake my head as we stop in front of Nathan's door. The door opens after I knock. Dad is standing there looking every bit himself against the backdrop of

Nathan's place. "She fell in the parking lot. She says she's fine, but I'm not sure."

"Let me help." Dad's expression isn't the one of concern I thought I might see. In fact, it doesn't change at all. What's wrong with him? Where is his compassion?

I push the struggles of my dad's emotions aside as I let him help Mom into the living room. Chills run through me as I realize I'm standing in Nathan's place. It's clean, contemporary, simple yet elegant.

High-end features of course. I knew that would be the case.

Big windows with a city view.

As I peruse Nathan's home Dad has settled Mom on the couch. She makes a great show of propping her foot on a pillow on the end table.

With her shoe on.

I rush over. "Geez. Take your shoe off. This is a pillow from his couch. People will sit with it."

Setting my keys on the coffee table next to her foot, I slowly maneuver her shoe off her foot and set it on the floor. "Your ankle looks okay. It's not swollen."

"I didn't do anything to my ankle. It's the side of my foot, but it's feeling better already."

"Everything okay?"

Sweat joins my chills at the sound of Nathan's voice. He's home.

CHAPTER THIRTEEN

I KNEW IT.

Maybe I wanted this to happen, you know, deep down inside. Although if that were really true, you think I would have changed my clothes.

Right?

Gorgeous Suzanna I am not right now.

"Emma fell in the parking lot. We're just making sure she's okay."

Dad speaks with authority and volume. Like he's acting in a play.

Weird.

There's so much about him I don't even know.

"I'm fine. This is entirely too much fuss being made over a little thing. A few minutes of rest and I'll be top-notch again." Mom is now firmly settled on Nathan's couch.

At least I had her shoe off before he came in.

I stand, brushing the few strands of hair that have escaped my bun away from my face. I turn my barely made-up face toward Nathan. "Hello. I'm sorry. We look like we're making camp here in your place, don't we?"

How, in a short time, has my family, in its entirety, invaded this man's space with such force? I mean we're all here, like we own the place.

The gorgeous, contemporary place.

A place I'll never be a part of. I've seen to that.

"You are fine. I'm sorry to hear about your fall. Do you need anything?" Nathan has walked over to where Mom is sitting.

He's dressed for work, his nice slacks and long-sleeved shirt reminding me of the night I first met him. I blush knowing what amazingness is under that shirt.

What kind of cruel fate is this?

I shouldn't have come here.

"I feel bad for leaving you. Are you sure you don't want to go to the doctor?"

Her expression does look pained, but she waves her hand in the air, brushing me off. Totally. "Nonsense. I don't need a doctor."

"I'll keep an eye on her this evening. I promise to let you know if it becomes worse."

I swear I see Mom roll her eyes at Dad's words.

Something weird is going on. I just don't know what it is.

Neither one of them have a car, so they aren't going anywhere.

But I am. I have to get out of here.

Away from Nathan.

Seeing his place makes him more real. More unattainable. He's so put together.

I'm so all over the place.

He has an amazing family.

Mine is dysfunctional right here in his living room.

"Call me when you are ready for me to pick you up." I kiss her on the cheek and wave goodbye to Dad.

And Nathan.

They all watch me leave. I feel their eyes on my back as I slip out the door. Pushing the down button once I reach the elevators, I cross my arms, tap my foot wondering how long elevators take in this swanky place.

I hear a door shut, but I don't look, fearing it will be Nathan.

I don't have anything to say to him.

Thankfully, the elevator softly dings then opens.

Pushing the button that says Lobby, I lean against the elegant elevator wall. Just as the doors are about to close, a hand prevents the doors from totally shutting.

And of course Nathan steps in.

I kind of smile but not really.

This is too much.

The doors shut.

His cologne softly envelopes me. Just like he has.

Whether I want to admit it or not, he has captured me.

My heart.

And I don't know what to do or how to act.

"You forgot your keys." He dangles them in front of me.

His words are like rain on my sunshine. Of course there is a perfectly logical reason for Nathan to have followed me into the elevator. Not some crazy, I-just-can't-help-myself-reason.

No. A sensible, practical, tangible reason.

I step forward grabbing them. "Thank you."

As soon as I fold the keys into my hands, he pushes the stop button. The elevator jerks before all movement stops. "What are you doing?"

"I have a feeling as soon as those doors open you'll bolt. I wanted to talk to you."

"Is this legal? Stopping the elevator for a conversation?"

He smiles. "Not sure. I wanted to explain the friend thing."

"Friends. Yeah. Sometimes friends are good, I guess. I'm not sure this is one of those times, though." I force a half laugh, trying to make light of the situation. It's embarrassing enough as it is.

"The thing is, I like you."

I take in his words. Really take them in.

Like.

It's a good word.

An appropriate word for a man wearing business clothes. A man with a highly intelligent brain. A man that is more gorgeous than he knows.

A man with a generous heart and an amazing body that houses it.

I'll take it.

My heart will take it. "I like you, too."

"I'm not my brother. I'm nothing like him and I never will be."

"Thank God."

His gaze searches mine. "I want to believe you. And kiss you. Again."

Oh, my heart. "Believe me and kiss me."

"People who are just friends don't stand in stopped elevators kissing. Do they?"

"There's always a first for everything."

"I like the way you think."

"I love the way you kiss." I know I am egging him on, but the attraction is more than I can take. Seriously, Nathan has my mind in a place it's never been before.

And I like this place.

Very much.

He places his hands on my shoulders. My skin trembles at his touch, my lips quiver in anticipation. I move closer to him, not closing my eyes as I want to see everything. I want to experience all of who he is. Every bit of his amazingness.

Looking into his eyes, I thought I was prepared for his lips meeting mine, but no.

Softly, he kisses me. So gentle that I yearn for more.

I drop my keys so my hands can hold tighter to hips. Tears threaten at the completeness I feel.

His kiss deepens.

I literally feel my knees shake, so I step back, pulling him with me, my body finally coming to rest against the elevator wall.

Running my hands up and down his sides, I don't want our kiss to ever end. Trapped forever in an elevator never sounded so good.

He breaks our bond, his breathing heavy, yet fast. "I think we are giving security quite the show." Moving quickly, he pushes the button, and the elevator starts moving. He stays close to the buttons. Far from me.

At least it seems far.

"I didn't think of that." I pushed strands of my hair away from my face before picking up my keys off the elevator floor.

"I thought of it a little late."

I stand, shaking my head. "I'm glad it took you a minute."

The doors to the elevator open. We walk out, curious stares coming our way. I totally get it. I'm dressed like I just left the gym, while Nathan looks every inch of GQ.

Well, the financial planner version of GQ.

"I'm in the parking deck."

He follows me to the elevator, but no kissing happens as there are others on there with us. We silently walk to my car. I juggle my keys from one hand to another, not sure what to say to Nathan.

He likes me.

I like him.

I work with his brother.

Nathan is giving my father a place to stay because he's broke.

Nathan just wants to be friends.

"Things got crazy last night. Again I'm sorry." He speaks as I push the button to unlock my car.

"Again, you have nothing to be sorry for. Things were going in a direction that they probably didn't need to be going in." I remember being out of my mind, tossing his shirt on the couch. Then his glasses.

Then he left.

"It takes two."

"Yes, it does. Then you went another direction. Which was for the best. We were very intense considering we are just friends."

I look at him.

Our gazes lock.

"We have to start somewhere." He shoves his hands in his pockets. "I'm not very good at this."

Smiling, I open my car door. "You don't need to be. I am the queen of dating advice in Atlanta. Just follow my lead."

"You can be dangerous for me, you know. Ned insists you'll rip me apart then feed me to the lions. He told me stay far away from you."

My throat suddenly dry, I don't know how to respond. What was Ned thinking talking to Nathan like that? "You don't always listen to your brother, I take it."

"No. I don't. Even though he is older."

"Speaking of older, what are my parents doing tonight? Mom didn't invite me to go with them. She just told me she had something to discuss with Dad. It's weird."

He runs his index finger down my arm. "Well, since they have plans, why don't we go grab some dinner. My treat."

I point to my hair and look down at my clothes. "I'm not going anywhere in this. Sorry."

Now he holds his index finger up. "One hour. Meet me at that new tapas place, Sorayas."

He doesn't give me time to protest. He turns and slowly jogs toward the elevator.

And I watch.

Unashamedly, I watch.

It's a very nice sight.

As he disappears around the corner it dawns on me that I have a lot to do in an hour.

I'M ONLY TEN minutes late.

I consider that an amazing feat.

He's waiting for me at the bar. When our gazes lock, he slides off his chair, meets me halfway, lightly brushing my lips with his.

Oh, why are we in a public place? Oh, because we are friends. I forgot.

He holds the back of the bar stool as I sit.

Such a gentleman.

"The bartender will be right back. She had to grab a key from the manager."

"That's fine. Have you eaten here before?"

"No. But I've wanted to. And you gave me the perfect excuse to try it."

"I'm sure you don't need a date to go out to eat, do you?"

"This is a date?"

My face flushes. "Strictly a friend date. But if you think differently. . ." I know there is tone to my voice now. A tone I don't like. But I'm embarrassed.

"Hey, I'm messing with you. I'm not all serious all the time. Relax." His hand rubs my back and I feel the tension lessen.

Gently, he turns my face toward his. He kisses me. A soft yet lingering kiss lasting not nearly as long as I would have liked it to. Sliding onto his barstool, he grabs my hand. "You are the prettiest friend date a guy could want. I'm no fool."

My heart is happy. It's like I can picture a future with Nathan. That is a thought I've never thought about anyone else I've dated. Even though he wants to call it friends, I'm calling it dating.

He doesn't have to know.

What's the worst thing that could happen?

My heart breaks into millions of pieces, that's all. I guess that's the risk you take when you start dating someone.

Dating. I should be taking notes for my job. What the heart feels like when it's happy. But really, how can one explain it? The feeling is almost too perfect for words. And again, he thinks we are friends.

"What can I get you?"

I turn as I see a white napkin being pushed toward me. I look up and gasp. "Riley?"

"Suzanna?" Her gaze darts between me and Nathan.

I point behind the bar. "You're working here?"

She pushes her hair behind her ears. "Yes, I am. Nothing wrong with a girl making some extra money, right?"

Her expression is nervous. Another couple approaches the bar. "I'll be right back." Riley goes over to the new couple, sliding white napkins in front of them as if she's on auto-pilot.

"You know her, I take it." Nathan sips his drink.

"Yes. She was on Love Atlanta Style with me. And now we are good friends. But not as good as friends as I thought, apparently. I just had lunch with her. I had no idea she had a second job. As a bartender."

"Maybe she just got the job. Or maybe she doesn't want anyone to know about her job." Nathan cocks his head like he's trying to make a point.

And I see his point. She has no idea about my new job. But it's not because I don't consider her a trusted friend, it's because I'm not sure how accepting she'll be.

151

With the attitude I have right now, maybe that's why Riley didn't tell me about her bartending job.

I'm not acting very accepting right now. "I'm just surprised, you know? There's nothing wrong with being a bartender. Especially in a place like this." My words are whispered as Riley pours two glasses of red wine for the couple sitting a few of stools down from us.

"I take it this isn't her normal occupation." Even though Nathan keeps his voice low, I know Riley knows we are talking about her.

"She's Prescott Wentworth's executive assistant."

Nathan's eyes widen. "Wow. He's a force in this city. A well-respected name in the business world and quite popular with the ladies from what I hear."

"That's what I hear, too. But Riley never says a word about him personally. She does love working for him, though. I wonder why she needs extra money."

Riley has set the wine down and is making her way back to us. Before she reaches us, the couple calls her back over.

"Excuse me, but is this Merlot? It doesn't taste like it."

Riley sidetracks back toward them. "I'm pretty sure. Let me double check." She walks over, then picks up the bottle. "Oh. I'm sorry. This is actually Shiraz. How did I do that?" She then takes their glasses and slides new glasses in front of them. She grabs a different bottle and seriously studies the label. She turns the bottle toward the couple. "Merlot. Promise."

She pours the wine into their glasses.

Her face is flushed and I can tell she's embarrassed. The couple smiles and continues talking, obviously not bothered by her mistake.

Riley arranges the bottles before coming back to Nathan and me. "Hi again. Did you want some wine, Suzanna?"

"I would. You know me well. Chardonnay please. Good Chardonnay."

"Of course."

She gives me a really full glass. There are perks to knowing the bartender. "How long have you been working here?" I ask.

"Not long."

Okay. It's going like that. I'm going to have to dig deep here to get any information from Riley. "Is this why you couldn't come to Farrah's engagement party? You had to work?"

"Probably. That was a last week right? I think I just started here. Bad move to call out when you're new."

Two guys sit on the other side of the couple and Riley heads over to them. I watch them check her out. Riley is the "girl next door" for sure. Beautiful, yet sweet.

"You don't know much more than you did when you walked in." Nathan places his hand on my knee.

I like it. It's like he's saying we are united.

"So, Riley is the friend that ditched Grace and me the night you and I met."

He nods. "Oh. Okay. It sounds like she hasn't had this job very long. Probably why she poured the wrong wine. She's new and maybe you are making her nervous. Not intentionally of course, but you know, having your friend around when you are trying to work. . ."

"Yeah. It would be like you looking over my shoulder while I tweet my dating advice. I'd probably give all the wrong advice."

"But that wouldn't be because you are nervous. That would be because I am a distraction."

"A good distraction."

"I'm glad you think so."

I think a lot of things about Nathan. A lot of things I probably shouldn't be thinking about.

CHAPTER FOURTEEN

NATHAN AND I walk into his place.

Mom is sitting on the couch watching a rerun of *The Golden Girls* while Dad is sitting at the dining room table eating a bowl of cereal.

They are in two separate worlds.

The television is loud, which explains why neither of them heard us come in.

I wonder what Mom needed to discuss with him. Apparently, they have discussed it.

And now they want nothing to do with each other.

My hand brushes Nathan's.

My body trembles momentarily. There will be no kissing tonight. Not with my parents here.

I start to walk away from Nathan's closeness. Before I can reach the couch Mom stands as a commercial comes on. She walks to the bathroom without issue. Not one sign of a limp.

Not once holding onto anything.

Nope. She boldly walks into the hall then shuts the bathroom door.

I look at Nathan. He looks puzzled as well.

We are still undetected by Dad.

Nathan grabs the remote and mutes the television.

That catches Dad's attention. He turns, spoon halfway to his mouth. "Oh, hi."

"Hi," I say. I nod toward the hall. "I guess Mom is okay? Her foot is fine?"

He does look a little confused, but only for a minute. He nods. "Oh, yes. She is fine. Must have been a little twist or something."

"Or something. Did you have your discussion?"

He looks puzzled. "Discussion?"

I shake my head. "That's what I thought. What have you two been doing since we left?"

"Your mother's been watching that fool show. Can't get her from out in front of that TV."

Mom comes out of the bathroom. She sees Nathan and me, and her gait changes. She's now got a slight limp.

"What's going on? We saw you walk to the bathroom just fine."

Mom continues what I'm sure is a charade of her fake limp. "It comes and goes. Fine one minute, sore the next. Hard to explain."

She makes a great show of barely making it to the couch. "Whew. Made it."

I sit next to her. "Why did you fake a sprained ankle? And don't deny that you are faking it."

"I have no reason to fake anything. It's sore and I'm sorry if you don't believe me. And there are times that I need someone with me. In California I'm all by myself."

"So this is a ploy to get me to move to California?"

"Move to California?" Nathan's tone is one of protest.

My heart soars.

The hustle and bustle of *The Golden Girls* on the television reflects the verbal chaos going on in Nathan's living room. "I told you, I'm not moving to California."

"That's fine if you feel okay leaving a woman to struggle her way through life all alone."

"Oh, brother. You are hardly struggling and no amount of fake ankle sprains will change my mind. Let's go. We've intruded on Nathan far too long now."

"You are never an intrusion." Nathan's voice calms me.

That's a nice feeling, especially after his kisses caused such havoc. "No, just a friend."

I know I have that snarky tone to my voice now, but Nathan has me confused and Mom has me on edge. She is playing some sort of game, and I'm not sure how she thinks she is going to convince me to move across the country.

It's not happening.

I SPEND WEDNESDAY at the office. Sonny has everything arranged for the television spot, we've signed the contracts, and he's spending extra time and effort to make sure Friday night is a success. After all he's booked the Coach Room.

I'm not sure I have a dress worthy of such elegance.

Because today Sonny informed Ned and me that this is a black tie affair for us. Not the public, but us.

Great.

I've only seen the Coach Room because that's where Love Atlanta Style holds their peach ceremonies. Every week we'd gather there to have our name called. If we were let go, we took the town car back to the hotel, packed our bags, and went home.

And it's not like I have any of the dresses I wore for those ceremonies. I had rented them all. No way could I afford those kinds of dresses.

158

Maybe I'll just go rent another one.

It's only for one night.

It's not like I'm going to be going to these types of events on a regular basis.

"Okay you two. Looks like we have everything set for Friday night. Be here by three. We'll go over everything one more time. Then you'll have hair and makeup. We're going all out for this, and it'll pay off big time. I can feel it." Sonny doesn't even say goodbye. He just walks out of the door of the conference room.

"I'm stoked." Ned pushes his chair away from the big table we've been sitting at for hours pouring over the logistics and plans for Friday night.

"I'm sure you are. Why did you tell Nathan to stay away from me?"

Ned's perplexed look does seem genuine. "I told him that?"

"He said you did."

"Sorry. I don't really think you two are compatible. I wasn't aware you were interested in my brother. I thought you were more interested in. . ."

"In?"

His face flushes slightly as he shrugs. "Nothing. I can't see you two together, that's all."

"He's an amazing kisser."

Ned points his finger at me. "There you go. That's one reason. Nathan would never kiss and tell. I knew it. I knew you two had gone past the friend zone."

Friend zone. Was Nathan using Ned's words when he talked about being friends? "Is that what you told him? That we should just be friends?"

"Suzanne. He's a numbers guy who thinks the term nightlife means staying up reading past dark. He was out the other night because he was doing me a favor. That's not who he is. And that is who you are."

"How can you claim to know anything about who I am? You can't even remember my name."

"He better remember your name. You two have a date tonight."

Sonny has walked back in. I wonder how much of our conversation he overheard? This is too much.

"What do you mean?" Ned asks.

"Brittany Benson is throwing a small shindig at the Adams tonight. Rooftop. And you two are there. She requested it. Kind of a segue into Friday night. Cocktail attire. You two arrive together, you leave together, you smile at each other a lot, you have great body language together. You ooze togetherness. Understood?"

160

"He can't remember my name."

"Suzanna. Uh. Uh. I've got it. Excuse me for the slip of the tongue a minute ago." He drapes his arm across my shoulders. It feels like lead.

Nothing like being touched by Nathan.

But this is what I wanted. This is my list of the perfect guy wrapped up in one man. Good looking. Single. Social. Carefree. Great job. Ned Parks has it all. And he's mine for the night. I should be feeling like Cinderella at the ball right now.

Instead I feel like my fairy godmother changed all the rules at the last minute.

I WAS QUITE surprised when Ned showed up in a limousine. Thank goodness I told him I'd meet him downstairs. Mom didn't need to know this bit of information. Ned probably would have mentioned it straight away seeing how he was so proud that he managed to secure permission from Sonny.

Ned's not paying for the limo.

He talked nonstop all the way here. I couldn't tell you half of what he said. I kept wishing he was wearing black-rimmed glasses.

The hotel valet opens the door. Ned exits first then is every bit the gentleman in helping me out.

I walk through the lobby of the Adams, Grace's father's hotel. I've grown to love this place and often call it my second home. Grace, Riley, and I have had our share of drinks at the bar talking over life, love, and the lack of love.

Brushing those memories aside, I stay close to Ned as we approach the elevator that will take us to the rooftop.

We are alone during the ride up.

"You look absolutely stunning tonight."

I try to let my heart react. But it doesn't. "Thank you. You look great yourself."

"We do make a nice-looking couple. Who wouldn't want to be us?"

Me. I don't want to be me right now. "I'm sure there are plenty of people happy with their lives. We are for the ones still looking. You match them up, I'll give advice. Teamwork."

With those words, the elevator opens and we step onto the rooftop into luxury. Brittany Benson, or her higher-ups, have gone way out for the event.

Space heaters are placed strategically around as May nights can still be chilly in Atlanta. Waiters and waitress carry trays laden with h'ordeurves and champagne. Obviously the term intimate means something different for Brittany than it does for me. There are at least a hundred people here already.

And we are only five fashionable minutes late.

"Suzanna, Ned. So great to have you join us. This makes the night complete, for sure." Brittany hugs each of us as she is speaking.

"We're stoked to be here," Ned says pulling me closer to him. "Thanks for the invite."

"It wouldn't be an event without you two here. The newest, latest, greatest Atlanta couple. Taking your own advice and making it work. I'm excited about Friday night. We're going to rock the city. Love stories coming true all over the city that night. Especially as everyone sees your very own love story playing out in front of them."

My mind is scrambling at her words. Latest, greatest couple? Latest, greatest working couple, maybe. "What we don't do for our jobs, huh?"

"And Suzanna and I are thankful for our jobs bringing us together. Who would have ever thought it could happen?" He kisses the top of my head.

I jerk my head at the foreign feel of his lips on my skin.

He's not Nathan.

Nathan. Who I didn't tell what I was doing tonight. I told him I had to work. Which is truth. But I didn't tell him what kind of work I was doing.

"Brittany. Can we get a photo?"

We all turn to see an Atlanta Unleashed photographer.

"Sure."

Brittany stands next to me, snuggling close. Her arm snakes around my waist like we are best friends. Ned's arm is draped across my shoulder in a protective, possessive kind of way.

To say I want to flee is an understatement. Multiple flashes momentarily blind me before giving everything I look at a blue halo around it.

"More guests are arriving. Y'all go eat, drink, and mingle. I'll catch up to you later. I am telling everyone about the event Friday night. Can't wait."

With those words she's off greeting the small crowd that just exited the elevator. I guess we weren't fashionably late enough.

"What was that kiss about? You don't kiss me."

"Together. That's what Sonny said."

"There's something going on here. Something I'm not privy to."

"Suzanna! Ah! You're here."

Grace rushes over, leaving Justin to catch up.

I have never been so glad to see somebody. "Hi." We hug and I instantly feel better. Whatever Ned is up to, I can handle with Grace here.

Ned and Justin shake hands. "Ned Parks."

"Sure. I remember. We met last week. Justin Walker."

"Oh, yes." Ned nods like he's remembering, but I wouldn't place money on it.

"We stopped by the hotel to say hi to Daddy and Wendy. They sent us up here to crash the event. In a good way, of course."

"He and Wendy are obviously still seeing each other."

"They are. She's really great for him. I still miss Mama every day," she holds up her arm, the bracelet her

165

mom gave her dangling daintily on her wrist, "but I'm glad to see Daddy happy. And smiling. He's always smiling now."

"That's good. You and your dad both found love."

She grabs Justin's hand. "We did. And we're hearing kind of the same thing about you and Ned, here. True love? I'm thrilled for you. Although I can't believe I had to hear it from Brittany Benson before I heard it from you."

Ned squeezes my shoulder like he knows I'm about to go off on some tirade.

He's right.

It's one thing pretending in front of people we don't know, but it's another when it's one of your best friends standing in front of you. "We are pretending. For a work function. And we're just pretending to like each other. We are not a couple." And now I've put my foot in my mouth regarding my job that I haven't told Grace about yet.

Grace's eyebrows raise. "Oh. That's not the news going around. According to all in the know, you two are the newest, greatest couple in togetherland. Although I must say I was a bit confused considering we had drinks with you and Nathan. Regardless, you know what you're doing. Some are expecting a proposal at the event Friday night. Is that the way things are going?"

I try to scoot out from under Ned's grasp, but he has a firm grip on my shoulder. This is not a good situation at all. Grace is not the only one confused.

"It's cool, Suzanna. Really it is. We just inspire great stories, that's all."

"Story is the key word here." I turn and look at him. "Where did this story start? And how much do you know about it?"

CHAPTER FIFTEEN

NED STARES BLANKLY at me. I've come to realize there's something to Ned's blankness. He's not as blank as he seems.

It's an act, I think.

"There may have been some talk. I never said I was on board, though. So don't blame me."

I literally remove his arm from my shoulder before taking a stance in front of him. "You need to start talking to me. Now. In my book, together doesn't equal proposal."

Ned holds his hands in the air as if he's dismissing any blame. "I'm all for saving somebody's job, but Sonny and Brittany were the ones cooking up the proposal idea."

"What do you mean saving somebody's job?" I realize people are starting to look our way, so I say the words quietly, like normal conversation, and I smile as I say them.

Such a farce.

But I'm finding out that might be Ned's MO.

168

"Nothing. I shouldn't have said that. Come on, let's have fun at this party and act like the happy couple we aren't."

For the first time I hear an edge to Ned's voice which calms me about any proposal. That's not happening. I need to find out more about whose job we are saving, and I have to tell Grace about my job.

But, she probably already knows. I guess I better fess up while I still can, let her know I'm not a girl who keeps secrets.

"So, I guess you've heard about my new job?" I kind of fold myself back into Ned's realm, scooting close to him like I might need an ally any moment.

"No. What job?"

Grace and Justin are holding hands, togetherness personified.

"Oh, I thought you might have heard since you knew all about the event Friday night. Although I'm sure you aren't going to be at the Coach Room. I mean the party is for all the singles in Atlanta and you two are about to set a wedding date, I'm sure."

"Stop trying to switch the focus here, Suzanna. Tell us about your job." Grace has a lilt to her voice like she's making light of our situation. But her eyes say different.

169

They say serious.

"I'm the gal operating the Love Atlanta Style Twitter handle. It's been great fun."

To say Grace's look is one of shock doesn't come close to describing her facial expression. She looks at Justin, then looks back at me.

Me, taking one step closer to the traitorous Ned.

But traitorous Ned seems safer right now than Grace.

"Wow. That's interesting. I had no idea. Really, none. And I'm going to apologize to you. Wow."

I don't think I've ever seen Grace at a loss for words, but she is now. "Why are you apologizing to me? You haven't done anything to apologize for. I should be apologizing about not trusting you enough to tell you about my job."

She probably remembers the words she spoke the other night saying how the advice was over the top. Her gaze won't meet mine which confuses me more than Ned confuses me.

My whole being, heart, soul, and mind wish Nathan was here. Not that he would change anything, but everything would change if he were by my side.

When I'm with him I feel like I can tackle anything that comes my way. And at this moment, Ned is crazy and Grace is acting weird.

Brittany walks up with two beautiful ladies. "Sorry to interrupt, but I have a couple of ladies here who are thinking about applying to be on Love Atlanta Style, season three. And since I have two alums here I thought you might be able to tell them what it is like being on the show and maybe answer some questions. Cassandra," she nods to the brunette on her left, "Tabitha," she nods to the blonde on her right. "Meet Grace Adams and Suzanna Worth, LAS alums from season one."

Grace and I shake hands with Cassandra and Tabitha. I'm on auto pilot, still confused about the conversation that was interrupted by Brittany.

Ned and Justin drift toward each other to avoid the extremely bubbly, girly conversation going on. Thankfully Grace does most of the talking. Not only is my brain still befuddled, but now I'm watching the female population starting to surround Ned and Justin.

I don't blame them. Honestly, those two guys could do a commercial for any male product, and it would sell off the shelves. They are that good looking.

Justin though, only has eyes for Grace. I watch him continually focus his gaze on her, while Ned doesn't ever look my way at all. He's got eyes for every one of the gals in front of him. Again, thoughts of Nathan come to mind.

Where would his gaze focus?

Would it be on me?

It better be.

And my world shifts.

Shifts to Nathan and his protective ways.

Nathan and his amazing kisses.

Nathan and his thoughtfulness.

Nathan and nothing else.

Warmth gently seeps its way through me. My heart feels at home.

I want to tell Cassandra and Tabitha to run as fast as they can away from Love Atlanta Style. Not because I didn't find love on the show, but because you find love where you least expect it. Like in a bar, waiting on a friend, trying to save face, and offering to pay someone to pretend they are your date.

And it dawns on me that I never gave Nathan his money.

And he's never asked.

That's because he's Nathan.

I bet with all my heart Ned would have asked.

"Don't you think, Suzanna?" Grace asks.

And I have no clue what conversation they were having. "Um, yeah." I nod.

Grace scoots closer to me. "See. Finding close girlfriends was my favorite part of the show. Otherwise, I would have never met Suzanna. And look at us, still hanging out two years later."

"That's nice." Cassandra looks bored with the conversation, like she doesn't want to talk about girlfriends.

"I see what you mean. I didn't know Cassandra before tonight, yet here we are, friends already I can tell, and now we meet you two, and I think we'll be friends. Am I right?" Tabitha looks hopeful as she speaks.

I do engage in this conversation. "Sure. Friends. Grace, why don't you have Justin take our picture? We'll tweet this moment into digital eternity."

It doesn't take much to draw Justin away from the crowd of females surrounding him and Ned.

Ned meanwhile keeps his stance and doesn't even know we are having our picture taken. We all smile,

Grace standing next to me, while I act like Cassandra and I are new best friends.

"All done. Take a look." Justin hands the phone to Grace. Cassandra and Tabitha ooh and ah over the pictures, while I think I look like an imposter. I know my smile is fake.

But I'm the only one who knows.

"It was nice meeting you, Cassandra and Tabitha. Good luck. I hope to see you on season three." Grace gently holds my arm, leading me away from the hopeful bachelorettes.

Justin follows and we are halfway across the rooftop deck before Ned catches up.

"Thanks for leaving me stranded." Ned can't pretend to look annoyed. He was having too much fun.

"If we weren't being paid for tonight you wouldn't have noticed. You either see dollar signs or females. I'm on to you." I try to make light of my voice, like I might be kidding. But I'm really not.

That is Ned totally.

Females and money.

That feels so shallow now.

Now.

AN.

After Nathan.

I'll be honest. Before Nathan I was all about men and money. Because I can't know what I don't know.

And I didn't know what it felt like to be in love.

Love.

That word again.

That word I wasn't sure I was ready for, but now that it is happening, I have no idea what to do. But Grace would.

Beautiful heiress Grace. So in love with Justin she'd probably give up her fortune. Not that he would ask, but I'm thinking that's how true love works. You are willing to sacrifice things you never thought you would in order to be all in with the one you love.

I know Sonny said I was supposed to stick by Ned, but I don't care. This is my life. My future. I don't want to mess it up.

Any more than I already have.

"Grace. Girls' room." I start walking, not giving Grace a chance to refuse.

I feel her by my side. We push through the door to the bathroom and thankfully there is a waiting area before entering the actual bathroom.

A plush waiting area of course.

Two overstuffed gold couches are pushed against walls covered in wallpaper that is reminiscent of the gilded age. Small, yet fancy, chandeliers hang from the ceiling, their low lighting casting shadows on the walls.

Sitting on one of the couches, I pat the seat next to me. Grace sits.

"I need advice." Might as well put it all out there.

"I'm probably not the best person to give advice." There's an uneasiness about Grace. That's unusual. She's normally confident and sure of herself. I'm not used to this.

"Trust me. You are the perfect person for this. I need advice on love."

I see her swallow hard as her eyes widen. "Love?" The word comes out all squeaky. Now I'm very concerned.

"Yes. Is that so hard to believe with me?"

She shakes her head. "No. Not with you."

"Then what? You look horrified."

Grace closes her eyes, like she's thinking.

Hard.

What could she possibly be contemplating? Maybe love is harder than I thought?

176

"I only want what's best for you." Her eyes have a pleading look to them.

"Isn't love the best thing? It seems to be for you." I am confused.

The dim lighting makes Grace look even more beautiful if that is possible. This is a room of beauty and the conversation contradicts the elegance.

"It is the best thing in the world when you find the right person."

Relief whooshes through me. I reach out and hug her. "I knew it." I refuse to put any credence on the fact that she doesn't hug me in return. I simply let her go. I'm not sure why she doesn't seem to be happy that I've found love.

But her physical and facial response indeed says she's not happy.

Or she's apprehensive.

Either could be true.

"I'm worried about you, Suzanna."

Now we are getting down to it. "Why? Never thought I'd be the type to settle down?"

"That's not it. It's a matter of who you are settling down with."

177

Now I'm confused. "I'm not sure where you are coming from. Especially since you don't know Nathan."

"Nathan?"

"Yes." Her look of confusion catches me up with her thoughts. "Oh. You thought I was in love with Ned. Uh, no."

"I can't tell you how happy I am to hear that. Girl, I thought you were going crazy."

I give Grace a hug and this time she hugs me back. "It's Nathan. I can't believe it's taken me this long to see it, but I guess hanging out with Ned has some perks. Compare and contrast."

"I really thought you were in love with Ned. I was going to call Riley for help with an intervention. Seriously."

Women coming in look at us like we are crazy, but I don't care. Pressing the corners of my eyes to stop the tears, happy tears, I pay no attention to what anyone thinks.

Just Grace.

And she looks happy.

For me.

"Now I know you are a good friend. You wouldn't just stand by and let me be with Ned without telling me how you feel. Honestly, that means so much. It does. I'm not sure I've ever had such a good friend. Mom will be relieved."

Thoughts of Mom and Tannery come to mind. Best friends.

"What? Your mom?"

I smile. "Yes. She's worried I don't have a best friend. She worries too much. And she wants me to move to California."

Grace shakes her head. "Are you moving?"

"No. Her best friend, Tannery, just died. Mom's lonely and came out here on a whim. I think Tannery's death really affected her. She's actually been hanging out with my dad, who's lost his fortune. Oh, I don't want to get into all this tonight. But just know that Nathan has been great. He's actually letting my dad stay with him. Because my dad has nowhere else to go."

"Oh, and your mom is staying with you."

"Yes."

"I can't wait to spend some time with you and Nathan. And speaking of spending time, I guess we better get out there to our guys. Well, my guy. And your pretend guy."

I stand and look in the mirror, making sure I don't have any mascara running down my face. I wish I had some blush I could brush on.

"You're beautiful, Suzanna," Grace says. She's standing next to me and in my opinion she's the real beauty. We are so opposite, Grace with her dark hair and eyes, and me with my blonde hair, bluish-green eyes.

She grabs my hand. "There is something I need to tell you though."

A slight shiver runs up my arm. She's holding my hand. Not a good sign. "What?"

She bows her head momentarily before looking straight at me. "When Ned said he was all about saving someone's job, that job is yours. Your Twitter job."

Gulping, I look at her. "What are you talking about? Sonny thinks I'm doing a great job. He told me so today. Ned and I are starting a television spot next week. We've already signed the contracts."

"Contracts are good. But someone reported to Sonny's boss that the Twitter handle was becoming too mushy, the advice was not thought out well. He's thinking of letting you go."

I pull my hand from hers. "I appreciate you caring, Grace, I really do. But I have to talk to Sonny. He told me to say what I thought was best. If there is some sort of script they want doled out, I'm all for it. He just needs to let me know. I wonder how many people have complained. It has to be a lot for him to consider letting me go."

"Or one very influential person."

"Exactly."

Grace's gaze meets mine. "I guess I have a lot of influence."

CHAPTER SIXTEEN

A NAUSEOUS FEELING hits my stomach. "Grace? You are behind this?"

"I had no idea it was you."

My eyes blink back fast tears. "I don't know what to say."

"I know I want to say I'm sorry. I'm going to talk to Sonny tomorrow. Tell him I'm all wrong. Now that I know it's you, I can see the beauty in your words. The you in your words. I feel terrible. Honestly, I do."

"I want to say all kinds of bad things to you, but I can't."

"You should. I would feel better."

"My mom would say I need to rethink this best friend status." Now all of my thoughts are jumbled. Going from extremely happy to upset and disappointed isn't good for the psyche. At all.

"I'm sorry, Suzanna. Really I am." Grace reaches for me, but I step away.

"I need to go. I'm being paid to be at this party, and I'm bringing new meaning to the phrase 'on break' by being in here so long."

Escaping the elegant waiting area doesn't take but a couple of steps. The door shuts behind me. I wish the range of emotions were behind the door as well, but they cling to me fast and hard, like a drenching rain.

A rain of betrayal.

It's not hard to spot Ned. Find the female crowd and you'll find Ned.

I work my way toward him, burying the crazy feelings threatening to ruin my life.

Not the feelings regarding Nathan. No, those I'll bury until I see him, because if I bring them to life right now, I'd leave this party, my work obligation, and find Nathan.

My parents might not have done everything right, but they did instill a good work ethic in me. And I'm not skipping out on my job.

We don't have much longer here anyhow. Might as well stick it out.

Besides, I need to know what Ned knows.

And how he thought he would save my job.

"Ah, here she is." Ned actually steps away from the women surrounding him to walk to me. I now know something is up.

"I've been looking for you," he continues. "Brittany wanted to talk with us."

"Great. Let's find Brittany then."

Ned says goodbye to his harem as we walk away.

"I was beginning to think you left me." His voice is low, but I can hear the tension in it. Ned probably isn't used to women leaving him.

"I don't cut out on work responsibilities. What did you mean by helping to save my job? I know that I might be getting fired, so how were you going to help?"

He sighs. "From what I was told, your firing wasn't a done deal. Sonny likes you a lot. The plan was to have me propose to you Friday night. Everyone would see how happy we are and that would give more credence to our jobs. Then later, we would break up, civilly of course, and show people how to 'break up well.' He had it all figured out."

"And Brittany knows?"

"Yes."

"Tell me, who didn't know all this? Oh, yeah, me."

"Sonny was supposed to tell you tomorrow."

184

"That's great. And tell everyone else today. Love that."

Ned is spared from reacting as Brittany walks up to us. "Hi. I have someone I want you two to meet."

We follow her. A table sits somewhat secluded from the others. There's a man and a woman sitting alone. As we come closer, I realize I know who this man is.

What I don't know is why Brittany is introducing him to Ned and me.

"Ned, Suzanna, this is Hallman Green of Hallman's Diamonds, and his lovely wife, Starla."

We all shake hands. I know of Hallman Green because he is the diamond guy for Love Atlanta Style. His diamonds are gorgeous.

And expensive.

It's a good thing the show pays for them.

"Suzanna and Ned, I'm afraid your secret has leaked to a couple of key people. So, you have an appointment at two tomorrow afternoon with Hallman. He's going to help you pick out the most amazing diamond for the big event Friday night."

At this point I'm wondering if Brittany is acting or if she thinks we are really going to get engaged. She has to know this is all for the job. Otherwise why would we have an appointment with the most expensive jeweler in town?

I don't know Ned's financial situation, but I'm not sure he can afford a Hallman Diamond on his own.

"This is a great honor, Mr. Green." Ned is eating every last bit of this up, while I want to throw up.

I have to talk to Sonny. I have to get this straightened out. I'm going along with everything for right now, but tomorrow, things will change.

As in, I might not have a job.

I'M THANKFUL THAT Ned is not as much of a gentleman as Nathan. Nathan would never let me go home from a party by myself. He would make sure I arrived home safely.

Ned had no trouble hailing me a cab when it was time to leave. Our limousine must have turned back into a pumpkin and disappeared for the evening.

He did hug me for show though and pretended to whisper sweet nothings in my ear. Those sweet nothings had to do with not being late for our ring fitting at two o'clock tomorrow. But after my meeting with Sonny in the morning we probably won't have that appointment.

I don't give the cab driver my address. I give him Nathans.

Of course I have to be buzzed in, so I ask the cabbie to wait while I see if Nathan is home. I purposely didn't text him. I wanted to be a surprise.

And he is surprised.

I pay the cab then ride the elevator to Nathan's floor.

As I step into the hall, I see him waiting outside his door. He's smiling and I'm glad I decided to do this.

"Come on in. Wow. You look beautiful." He stands to the side as I walk into his condo.

The television is on but the volume is low.

"Is my dad here?"

He closes his eyes and sighs. When he opens them pools of blue darken. "I thought you might be here to see me."

"I am. I just didn't want Dad interrupting me kissing you." I know my words come out sounding breathless, but I don't care.

I am breathless.

Nathan is gorgeous.

And a gentleman.

And really, everything I have been looking for.

Because I had no idea what I was truly looking for.

187

He welcomes me into his arms, his mouth meeting mine in a perfect fit.

He is perfect. We are perfect.

I press my body to his as my lips take in everything about him. My hands run through his hair, down his neck, across his shoulders. They want to be everywhere he is.

He breaks our kiss.

His index finger caresses me under my chin before tilting my head up. "What are you doing roaming the city in that beautiful dress. You look like a princess."

"And you're my prince." I don't want to talk about tonight. About Ned. About a possible stupid, fake proposal from Ned.

Ned isn't anyone's prince.

But I have to.

"Big party, huh?"

I shrug then kiss him.

Once again his lips leave mine. "Didn't invite me? I'm hurt."

"It was a work thing. Besides, do friends invite friends to fancy parties?"

Now he cups my face with his hands and kisses me. I could never get tired of Nathan's kisses. Never.

We are perfect for each other. I just need to make him see it the same way.

We stop kissing and walk to the couch. He sits before pulling me onto his lap.

"Where is my dad?" I whisper.

"In his room. He went in a while ago." He keeps his voice low, too. "I need to talk to you."

And I need to talk to him about Ned. I'm going to tell him all about how hanging around his crazy brother showed me the way to true love.

With Nathan.

I kiss his forehead, his nose. I don't even notice his glasses anymore. And when I do, I love them.

"I told you before, I'm not good at this dating scene. You go with the wind, Suzanna. I know we'll both be hurt before all is said and done. I'm different than you. Not better, just different. I'm structured, a planner. You are anything but structured. And your plans change with the wind. I'm not good at that."

"You're better than you think you are. Look how you took my dad in at a moment's notice. That wasn't planned. You cooked dinner for my parents in my condo, again unplanned. You're loosening up. And you're good at it."

189

"I'd like to think you are right. We all bend and move when we have to, but it's your way of life."

"I want my way of life to include you."

"I want that, too—"

I knew there was a "but" coming, so I didn't let him finish. Instead I placed my lips on his and kissed him in the sweetest way I knew how. My arms are wrapped around his neck.

In this moment he's mine.

All mine.

We stop the sweetest kiss in the world.

"I'm afraid you'll hurt me."

His words slice through the sweetness, real and raw.

I understand his fear. I feel it as well.

"I won't. Ever." I say the words, knowing they aren't a promise I can fully make. No one can see the future.

"I want to believe you. I want to love you."

"Like I said yesterday, believe me. Love me."

"I already do." He runs his index finger over my bottom lip. "I think about you constantly. All day, all night."

"I'm glad this is out in the open. I want to scream it to the world. I'm in love. Real, true love."

"Yes. You must tweet it so everyone will know." His tone is making fun, but reality crashes around me. I have to tell him about Ned and the fake proposal.

"There's something I have to tell you, though."

"Oh, no. This doesn't sound good. At all."

"It's about Ned. And work. It's all work."

"Go on."

"You know I told you we were hosting a party Friday night. He's going to do some matchmaking, and I'm handing out dating advice."

"Okay."

I take a deep breath. "Part of the party consists of Ned proposing to me."

"Proposing what?"

I hit him gently on the arm. "Marriage, silly."

"I just tell you I love you, and you then tell me my brother is going to propose to you and you call me silly? What am I missing?"

He does not sound happy.

"It's just for the job. Apparently Grace, who didn't know I was the gal behind the Twitter account, complained about the advice I was giving, so Sonny questioned my job performance. Sonny apparently doesn't want to fire me, but he does have to answer to the higher-ups, so he and Brittany Benson, the gal whose show we are going to be on, cooked up this plan. They think the reaction from the public will be great and my dating advice will be the talk of the town. It's confusing, I know."

"What's really confusing is if Ned does propose to you, how are you going to get out of that one? Or are you?"

I want to kiss away the anger in his voice. "Of course. They said we would just eventually break it off, but someone else will be in the news by then. I don't know."

"And you told them you'd go along with this crazy scheme?"

"I never agreed, but I didn't disagree. Ned and I are supposed to be at Hallman's Diamonds, downtown, at two tomorrow."

He's no longer relaxed. I can tell by the way he's holding me. It's like it's not natural. Like he's forcing himself to have me in his arms.

That's the last thing I want to happen.

"I'm going to the office tomorrow and tell Sonny that the proposal is off. Or I'm quitting."

"Suzanna. I don't want you to quit your job over me."

"It wouldn't be over you. I don't want to be Ned's fake fiancée. I guess I was scared that I might lose my job if I protested too much. Then my mom will have one more reason for insisting I move to California."

"You aren't moving anywhere. That sounds Neanderthal, doesn't it? You know what I mean."

"I do. And I'm not moving. Anywhere. I may not even have to quit. Because of my best friend, Grace, I might get fired. I texted Sonny that I want to see him tomorrow morning."

"Nobody is going to fire you. That would be insane. And look, I know I'm acting stupid crazy right now, but I see women become enthralled with Ned all the time. I'm no competition for him."

"You're right. There is no competition. I love you."

"You won't do the fake engagement then?"

"No. Way. I'll handle all of that tomorrow. But for now. . ."

I want to concentrate on sitting in Nathan's lap, in Nathan's condo, in the semidarkness with his lips a mere breath away from mine. "You know I'm the happiest girl in the world."

"And I'm in a dangerous position. I've got the most beautiful girl in the world sitting on my lap and her father sleeping in a room right down the hall."

"I don't want to leave."

"I don't want you to leave. Not right now. This is what I want."

He kisses my chin, my neck. Warm kisses land on my shoulder before finding their way to my lips.

I know it's getting late.

I don't care.

I'm where I'm supposed to be for the rest of my life.

CHAPTER SEVENTEEN

SONNY CANCELLED THE meeting this morning. I texted Ned to tell him I couldn't meet him at two, but I never heard back from him.

So now, it's ten minutes until two and I'm on my way to Hallman's Diamond store to tell Ned the whole thing is off.

I look awful.

I don't care.

I stayed at Nathan's until after midnight before he drove me home, escorted me to my condo, and then kissed me forever.

That thought puts a smile on my face.

Then I couldn't sleep for thinking about how incredible it feels to be in love. I love the feeling, no pun intended.

And since I told Nathan about Ned last night, today I'll tell Ned about Nathan. I arrive at Hallman's, open the door, and come to a complete stop as I enter.

Lights and cameras are everywhere.

Did I mention I look terrible?

"Suzanna!" Brittany Benson greets me. "Hi." She points to her head. "Great minds think ahead. Hon, I've got my hair and makeup gals on call, just for you. How did you know? We also have a dress or two in wardrobe you can choose from. They'll be quick. We need to start filming."

I don't speak as Brittany hands me off to her girl crew.

I don't see Ned either.

"Brittany, can I talk to you for a minute?" I manage to say before she totally goes out of ear shot.

"Sure, just give me a sec. Let them start on your hair and makeup, though. We don't want to waste valuable time here."

I find myself in a back room slipping on a blue-green dress because they won't start on my hair or makeup until I take off my T-shirt. This is insane. I have no idea what's going on.

I don't take my gaze off the door. Surely Brittany will be in here any moment.

Any moment turned into moments, which turned into minutes, which turned into I walk out of the back room door before she walks in.

And I walk out looking amazing.

Amazing with the help of Brittany's help.

The diamond shop isn't in a big space. It's not tiny either but somewhere in between which would probably be a comfortable space except for all the lighting and cameras.

I do see Ned now. He's sitting with Brittany and Hallman. Great! This is my opportunity. And I look like a million bucks dumping the best matchmaker in the city.

"There's the girl of the hour. I'm sorry I didn't get into see you. I became caught up in conversation with these two guys here. Conversation about you as a matter of fact."

About me? All eyes are on me that's for sure. Ned's even have a sense of depth to them today. Like what he's about to do is important.

Like picking out an engagement ring for a fake engagement has some meaning. Well it doesn't and they are about to hear those words from me.

But his eyes in no way match his brother's. Nathan's eyes can carry me around the world. They can help me through the worst day.

They say I love you every time he looks at me.

"You have an agent, right?" Brittany asks me.

"Yes. Why?"

"I suggest you call her asap. Hallman here has an offer of a lifetime."

Hallman stands, his hands motioning for me to sit in his seat which is really a director's type chair brought in for today.

I sit, crossing my legs, for what I have no idea. Oh, yeah, the offer of a lifetime.

"What do you think of this?" Hallman hands me a red box in the shape of a heart. Velvet on the outside. A fancy heart-shaped clasp secures the lid shut.

I open it, touching the silky material inside. "I think it's beautiful."

"I thought you would. Say these words for me. "Hallman's diamonds. Where true love begins."

"What?"

"Hallman's diamonds. Where true love begins."

I repeat the words. Hallman chuckles. "Okay. Now say them like they are true."

Completely clueless I repeat the words.

We are sitting next to the store windows. People walk by oblivious to the craziness that is going on in here. Now and then someone will look in, but they quickly look away and keep walking.

"The words sound like diamonds falling off your lips." Hallman has a huge smile on his face after speaking.

"What is going on?" I ask to no one in particular, but hoping someone will answer me.

"I am looking for a Hallman's Diamond girl. And I think I have found her."

"Me?"

"Don't be surprised. You're beautiful, confident, bold. Everything I'm looking for in my diamond girl. You will be the girl to make this red box as famous as the blue box from Tiffany. What do you think?"

Hope springs inside me. "I think I might want to know more about this diamond girl job."

Hallman receives a call on his cell phone. "Excuse me for a minute. I need to take this." He steps away from us.

Ned and Brittany are staring at me. "Well, sounds great, doesn't it? He's talking a five-year contract. Big money." Brittany winks at me after she speaks.

Five-year contract? Immediately thoughts of Nathan come to mind. It's a plan. A five-year plan. I'll have a consistent, steady income for five years, and it won't involve having to pretend to be engaged to his brother. How perfect is this?

"This sounds too good to be true. And you know what that means. . ."

"He's on the up and up. He's been working behind the scenes for the last couple of years with a marketing firm putting together the right advertising blitz. He told me he's been searching for just the right girl for the last three months. He said he would know her when he saw her. You are her."

"I'm flattered." I couldn't have asked for anything better after my conversation with Nathan last night. "But what about the television spot?"

"Still on. Hallman knows about it. You'll be doing most of your filming here in Atlanta. My ratings are going to go through the roof."

Everyone is always looking out for themselves.

Hallman approaches us again. "I'm sorry about that. Couldn't be helped. Back to business. Regarding the Hallman Diamond Girl position, I'll have a contract forwarded to your agent if you are interested."

"I'm interested."

"Good. I think you and I are going to be a great team. Just like you and Ned, here."

"Ned?"

"Yes. All this publicity from you two, combined with the party Friday night and the engagement will propel this campaign."

"But." I stammer. I can't believe I'm stammering, but I am.

"But what?"

"Well, we all know the engagement isn't real. So what happens when we break up? How will that affect everything?" I try to keep my voice calm. I need to know all the facts before I boldly state I'm not going through with the fake engagement. I have to distance myself as far from Ned as possible, yet keep my Hallman Diamond Girl offer.

"We have all of that figured out," Brittany says. "Ned is going to propose to you, and you are going to accept, act happy, slip on the ring. Then, we are going to get a crowd reaction. Of course everyone will be ecstatic. Then we are going to announce that Ned wasn't really proposing to you, but it was still beautiful. And we'll tell everyone that they can have a beautiful proposal just like that if they buy a Hallman Diamond. What do you think?"

I'm thinking I don't know what to do. This is a bit of a different scenario. The engagement isn't going to even be real for a night. Just a minute or two. Probably less. That does shed a different light on things.

A light I might could go with. "What about Sonny? My Twitter job?" Will I even be able to keep my Twitter job?

"Sonny is cool," Ned says. "Apparently Grace met with him this morning and they worked everything out."

"That's good, I guess." Somehow I'll have to explain all this to Nathan. Surely he won't mind. "I think this might work. I'll have three jobs, but that's okay."

"Great." Hallman looks please. "Now let's start picking out the ring. We are going to film it for future use, maybe."

"And I'm using some footage Monday morning on my show before these two come on to do their two minutes." Brittany sounds happy.

While I've been wondering why we've been seeing so much of Brittany, I might have my answer. When she thinks no one is looking, I find her staring at Ned. Yes, Ned.

I think Brittany might have a thing for Ned.

I need to warn her away from him.

Certainly she can see what a player he is. But then again, I knew what a player he was, and it didn't bother me.

Until I saw what real love looks like.

Tastes like.

Acts like.

The director's chairs are moved away and Hallman goes behind the counter. He places a tray of rings on the sparkling glass counter after he asks what size my finger is.

My ring finger.

"We're ready to start filming," one of the guys says.

"Do your thing." Brittany steps out of the camera view as Hallman shows us different rings and explains them in detail. He picks up one that is exquisite. Breathtaking.

"Oh, I love that ring." My mind is filled with Nathan and what it would be like to have him propose to me. It would be awesome, and this ring would be a cherry on top.

"Let's try it on, then."

Ned holds my left hand, the engagement ring ready to slide on my finger.

"What's going on?"

"Cut!"

I turn at the sound of Nathan's voice. I want to be happy I'm seeing him, but his stance and demeanor doesn't say happy at all.

It says the exact opposite.

Pulling my hand away from Ned's, I walk to Nathan. I try and hug him, but he steps back. "What's going on here? I tried to call you, but you didn't answer. It's obvious you were busy."

"Um, yeah. Things are different than I told you last night."

"Different, how?"

"Hello, young man. Hallman Green. I'm sure you know you look just like our fellow Ned. And it looks like you know our new Hallman Diamond Girl." Hallman offers his hand.

Nathan accepts his offer, leaving me feeling more troubled. "Nathan Parks. Ned's twin."

"Twins. None in my family that I know of. Interesting when it happens, though. We're filming a reality segment here. Ned's proposing to our Diamond Girl on Friday night, and I think we just found the perfect ring."

Nathan's eyes say all the words he doesn't.

"I can explain."

He shakes his head. "That's quite all right. I think Mr. Diamond here said all that needs to be said." Nathan turns and walks out.

Ignoring the calls of Ned and Brittany, I follow Nathan and catch up with him outside the store. "It's only for a minute." I tug on his arm, turning him around to face me.

I notice that Hallman, Brittany, and Ned are watching through the window.

I don't care. I stammer on, "Sonny canceled the meeting this morning. So I came here prepared to tell Ned this whole thing is off, except as soon as I walk in here I am whisked into a back room, given a dress to wear, and had my hair and makeup done."

Nathan is listening, but I can tell I'm not making an impact.

"I mean, I finally have a chance to speak to everyone, and Hallman offers me a job of being the spokesperson for his diamond store. Brittany said he was talking about a five year contract. I thought of you. And how I can finally have a plan. A steady job."

"And the proposal? You said you would call it off."

"I was going to, but they changed the plan." I proceeded to tell him how the engagement was only going to last for two or three minutes tops. "So, see it's totally fake. All to be resolved that night. In less than five minutes."

Nathan shakes his head. "It's not about the proposal, really. It's happening again. You're going with the wind. The next best thing. A two-minute engagement now, what will be next? I get that it's not that big of a deal, but the big picture, Suzanna, that's a big deal. And this?"

He places my hand on his chest over his heart. "This is broken. I'm sorry, I have to go."

With those words he lets go of my hand then leaves.

I'm standing in the middle of the sidewalk in uptown Atlanta, Buckhead, tears streaming down my face.

And all the people walk by like it's normal.

I ARRIVE AT my condo on what should be a celebratory day. I probably have a long term job with Hallman's. Being their diamond spokeswoman was going to be an exciting job.

Until Nathan said goodbye.

Now nothing seems exciting.

And everything is awkward.

My dad is still staying at Nathan's, so I know we'll have some interaction. Nathan and I traveled from strangers to friends, to I love you, then to nothing in a short period of time. My emotions are exhausted.

I'm exhausted.

I want that sparkle back in my life.

Yes, I know it's only been gone a couple of hours, but I want it back.

I want Nathan back.

Ned told me he'd try to help out, but really, Ned will only make things worse. He doesn't get it.

Brittany gets it, but there's not much she can do.

Opening the door to my condo I just want to lie down and forget this entire afternoon. Maybe Nathan and I are too different. What I saw as a plan, he saw as me changing my mind, again.

Not following through.

But the scenarios were so different.

"Hello, Suzanna."

My dad is sitting on my couch. Mom is not.

"Hi. Where's Mom?" I don't want to talk about what happened this afternoon. I will keep the focus on them.

"She ran out for a few minutes. How are you?"

I raise my eyebrows. Dad doesn't ever ask that question, really. I mean he may ask it, but he expects the answer to be "fine" and we go on with the conversation. I wonder what would happen if I told him the truth?

"I'm great." I say the words with absolutely no enthusiasm.

None.

But this time he notices. "Come. Sit."

He pats the spot next to him on the couch. I do as I'm told. Not because I'm like a child all of a sudden, but because he is my dad. Moments like this haven't happened very often during our lives, and I want to savor them when they do happen.

"I know I haven't been around much. I've let a lot of people down in life. It took me too many years to figure that out. I want to say I'm sorry."

I want to believe him so badly. I know when people hit rock bottom they can change, and it can be a real change. But how do you know when someone has spoken empty words?

My face heats at the thought.

This is how Nathan feels.

My words last night meant nothing today.

Am I a product of my father, really?

208

I look at him. He's aged of course. His hair is more white than not. His face, wrinkled in all the right places, has stood the test of time more well than not. I take his hand in mine. "It's okay. You're here now."

And I want to believe those words. I want to believe he'll stay in my life now.

Of course he doesn't have three or four other houses to go to, but when it's all done, I realize I don't care why I have him here, I'm just glad I do.

"Thank you, Suze. I promise I've learned too much to go back to who I was."

Suze. He's is the only person that has ever gotten away with calling me anything but Suzanna.

"It's been too long since you've called me Suze. I think I've missed it. But don't tell a soul."

He smiles. "I won't. But I will tell everyone that you give great dating advice. It's worked for me."

"For you? When have I given you dating advice?"

"On your Twitter advice column thingy."

Heat rushes through me. "I've given you advice through Twitter?"

"Buildinglife? That's me."

I must say I already feel betrayed. "Why did you do that? Nathan said you were trying to win Mom back. Is that true? Were you asking advice for you and Mom?"

"I thought it was fun. You were being honest and straightforward. You gave me a lot of good advice. And yes, it was regarding your mother. I love her."

"Mom? No." I stand. First Nathan leaves me and now my dad is trying to do something he shouldn't have ever undone years ago.

And I've helped him.

Inadvertently of course.

I thought my day couldn't go further south, but it has managed to do just that.

Dad follows me. I'm staring out the window, avoiding looking at him.

"Suze, what's wrong with me trying to win your mother back? She's a great lady. I'm sorry for the past, but I can't change that. I can only change the future."

"I know exactly what you are saying. And frankly you haven't been good with sticking to your word. I'm afraid Mom is going to be hurt. She's already in a strange state because of Tannery's death. She's vulnerable right now. Please don't take advantage of that. Please?"

I see the change on his face. I want to take my words back, but they are truth. And I can't take back truth.

He looks down, pushing at the corners of his eyes with his fingers. "I want what's best for you and your mother. Again, I'm sorry for everything. I thought I could rebuild, but. . ."

I have trouble ignoring his shaky voice but this is serious. "Lives aren't buildings. We can't just be erected and torn down at someone's whims. It doesn't work that way."

"I see that now. I'll find somewhere to go and I'll let you know where that somewhere is. Tell your mother I said goodbye, will you?" He hugs me. I don't want to let him leave like this, but I know it's for the best.

"Tell me yourself, Jameson. I thought you had changed. I guess I was wrong."

Mom shut the door and as quick as she came in unnoticed, she left with a big notice.

And once again, I've made everything worse.

CHAPTER EIGHTEEN

MOM REFUSES TO talk about the Dad situation.

It's Friday morning. She's still sleeping but I endured hours of silence from her last night. The party is tonight. The party for which I have no enthusiasm.

How did I mess up everything so fast?

And all in one day.

I see how Nathan came to the conclusions he did yesterday. Like Dad, my words seemed to mean nothing to me as I was constantly contradicting myself with my actions. I have to figure this out.

I have to show Nathan that I meant my words of commitment to him.

But I may lose my job with Hallman if I go through with my plan.

Oh, well. There's always a price to pay, isn't there?

I'd rather have Nathan and no diamond job than to have the diamond job and no Nathan. I somehow, someway need to make sure Nathan is at the party tonight.

But he won't come if I invite him.

I'm sure of it.

Maybe Ned will help?

Brittany?

Grace?

Grace.

I text her to see if she's free for coffee. She answers with a smiley face, so I grab my purse, write a note for Mom, and leave.

Grace is already at our table with a coffee waiting for me when I arrive. We hug and tears flow from both of us.

"I'm sorry." We both speak at the same time.

"I shouldn't have talked to Sonny about the advice. I'm so sorry. Just because you don't give the advice I would give doesn't mean it was wrong. I can't believe I did that. Justin told me to stay out of it. I should have listened to him." Grace's words rush over each other in her reconciliation attempt.

It works.

I rub her arm. "It's okay. Really. My dad was tweeting me and now he wants to get back with my mom. Talk about bad advice."

"You gave your dad bad advice?" She laughs after she speaks in her fun, Grace way.

"He made a Twitter account. Of course I didn't know it was him. He did what I said to try to win my mom back."

"Did it work?"

I think on the hope I saw in his eyes last night, then the disappointment I heard in her voice when she overheard the end of our conversation. "I think it was working, but then I had a talk with him last night and told him to quit pursuing her."

"Oh. Speaking up for Mom, huh? She didn't want to hurt his feelings?"

Mom really thought Dad had changed. And she refused to talk all night. "You know, I didn't ask Mom what she wanted. I just know I didn't want Dad to hurt her again."

Grace nods in understanding. "You probably did the right thing. I tried to 'protect' my daddy from Wendy. We just want what is best for our parents."

I laugh. "Or what we think is best. I'm not sure why I could accept that Dad could change for me but not for her. I can't even keep my own love life straight. What makes me think I can speak for anyone else? Great, another problem I have to solve today."

Grace sips her coffee. "Another? What's going on?"

214

"I need your help."

She sets her cup down. "Sure. Anything."

I take a deep breath. "I've messed things up with Nathan. Badly. I need him at the big party tonight. Can you get Nathan there? I'll give you his number. I don't care what you tell him, just make sure he is there."

"Why can't you ask him?"

I explain to her everything that happened over the last two days. "Now, you see? My words don't matter to him. I need action. And I have the perfect plan. I just need him there."

"He'll be there. I promise. If I have to go and drag him myself I will. Actually, Justin will do the dragging. I don't think my muscles are strong enough."

We both laugh. "Thank you, Grace. You don't know what this means to me. All I know is I don't want to live without Nathan."

MOM IS UP and packing her suitcase when I arrive back at my condo.

"What are you doing?" I ask her this even though it is obvious.

"I'm going back to California. I know I can't convince you to move with me. And your father, well, he's gone off again. I really thought I could trust him this time."

"Mom, sit. Please?"

We sit on the couch, close to each other. No more distance. I'm tired of distance. I take her hand in mine. "Maybe you can trust him. I think he's changed."

"I heard him with my own ears, yesterday. He told you to tell me goodbye. I didn't make that up."

Shame washes over me at my attempt to save Mom. "No, you didn't. But. He was only saying that because I told him to leave you alone. I believe he had changed when it came to me, but for some reason I couldn't see the same for you. I was wrong. He has changed. And if you like what you see, I'm sure that's who he is now."

"I want to believe he's a changed man. He was never a bad man, he was just a man with priorities that I thought weren't in line with mine. Ours."

"He sees what's important now. I believe he does. And I'm sorry for anything that I've said that caused this barrier between you."

She smiles. "He said he followed your Twitter advice."

"Isn't that crazy. I can't believe I didn't know. Here I am, love life a mess, and I'm giving my dad advice."

"What's going on, Suzanna? What happened?"

"Nothing that can't be fixed." I hope. I pray.

I reach over her and grab Tannery's book. I open to the page with the poem. "Listen to what Tannery wrote. 'Hearts filled with emptiness, lives that are just a mess. Broken roads and shattered dreams, nothing is ever as it seems. I run, I walk, I try to fly, but I never really reach the sky. Then comes along my saving grace, kissing me gently, cupping my face. His hands so strong, his heart so sure, for a moment I think he is my cure. Then darkness falls as he leaves me here, I find I shed just one tear. Not two, not three not any more. Than one, for my love walked out the door.'"

My mom has tears in her eyes. "Tannery didn't write that. I did."

Surprise and shock settle over me. "What?"

"I wrote it years ago when your father left. Tannery loved it. Thought it was very poetic and tragic. Beauty and darkness wrapped in one, she said."

I feel now like I haven't known Mom at all. That has to change. "Grab your beauty, forget your darkness. Please? And instead of me moving to California, would you think about moving back here?"

A thoughtful look passes over her. Then she kisses me on the cheek. "I'll think about it. I like the idea."

I'M WEARING A beautiful strapless gown in a blue color that accentuates my eyes. And I didn't even have to rent it. Brittany hooked me up. My hair is full and curled and sprayed. I don't think a hurricane could move it. My makeup is perfection, of course, according to Brittany's makeup gal.

Everyone is telling me I've never looked so beautiful, yet I don't feel beautiful inside. I feel torn, strange and almost sick at what's going to happen tonight. I decided not to tell Ned my plan. He will tell Brittany, I'm sure, and she will try to stop me.

And I'm totally counting on Grace to bring Nathan here so I can show him that I'm a girl who stands behind her words.

A girl that loves him.

A girl that won't change her mind like the wind.

A girl that will commit to him.

Ned walks up to me. We are in a back room about to go out and mingle with the masses. The single masses.

"Ready?" he asks.

"I am." I have never been more ready.

"You look amazing. If I thought I had a chance, I might be sincere in my proposal tonight."

"You don't have a chance." From the outside, Ned has to hit every girl's wish list. Built, handsome, perfect hair, great complexion. But looking at him now, I see the differences between him and Nathan.

Nathan's face holds compassion. Nathan's gaze doesn't wander. Nathan's heart is true, pure, and for one woman.

Ned buttons his tuxedo jacket. "I tried to talk to Nathan last night. He wouldn't return my calls. I wanted to tell him how great you were and that he was being stupid."

Ned looks sincere as he speaks. I squeeze his arm. "Thank you. I appreciate that."

"Don't give up on him, yet. I'll work on him."

"I'm not sure I want a guy you have to work on."

We both laugh, yet it's true. If I can't convince Nathan I'm his girl, no one can.

Or should.

Then darkness falls as he leaves me here
I find I shed just one tear.
Not two, not three not any more,
Than one, for my love walked out the door.

Uptown Flirt

My love may have walked out the proverbial door, but I refuse to shed even one tear.

Because he's going to walk back in.

He has to.

CHAPTER NINETEEN

I'M TIRED OF smiling.

And it's only been thirty minutes.

I've been sipping on the same glass of champagne the whole time. The bubbly drink tastes good, but I have to be clear headed. And sometimes champagne gives me a headache. I don't want a headache now, although the tension I'm causing inside myself might give me one anyway.

There is no sign of Grace or Justin.

Or Nathan.

In five minutes Ned and I are headed on stage to do our thing. At least that's what he thinks. I have another thing I'm going to do. But Nathan has to be here. Whether he's here or not though, I'm going through with my plan. I have to do it for me.

Brittany walks up to me. "It's time."

She links her arm through mine, and we walk to the stage, Ned following.

The Hallman Diamond display is centered on the stage, the big backdrop for the proposal.

I will say I'm nervous. My hands are starting to sweat. A handler takes my glass of champagne as Brittany and I walk up the stairs. As we reach the stage I scan the crowd. There are too many faces with no way to determine if Grace, Justin and Nathan are here. My heart beats fast, knowing I'm about to break all the rules.

But for love, are there really any rules?

Ned and I stand to the side as Brittany takes the microphone.

"Welcome! Hello, everyone!"

There are shouts and cheers. Everybody loves Brittany Benson. It's obvious by the size of the crowd as well as their reaction to her.

"I know you are all having a great time. And I know love is in the air!"

Another round of shouts and applause.

I hope the crowd is as enthusiastic at my change of plans.

Brittany waves her arm to her right where Ned and I are standing. "How about a Brittany welcome for our very special guests tonight, Ned Parks and Suzanna Worth."

Ned and I step forward as the crowd gives us a crazy good reception.

"Suzanna, come over here."

Ned leaves my side as Brittany wraps her arm around my waist. "I wanted to say a few words about Suzanna. She's no stranger to Atlanta. Besides recently appearing on Love Atlanta Style, she is the voice behind the Twitter handle 'dating Love Atlanta Style.' Let's give it up for all the great advice she's been giving to the singles of Atlanta."

Another round of applause.

"And now, we have a special surprise for you tonight. It seems a couple of our singles might be off the market. I hear there is a proposal in the air tonight. What say you, Atlanta!"

Now the roar is deafening. My stomach feels like it's in my throat which is dryer than it's ever been. I need water.

I need strength.

I envision Nathan.

I breathe deep. I can do this.

"Suzanna, I believe there's a gentleman who has something to say to you."

I shut my eyes as Brittany steps away.

I turn toward Ned, who I know from practicing earlier, will be on one knee.

I look down at Ned, but something is off.

It looks like Ned in his tuxedo, but the eyes. They're blinking fast, and they're not Ned-blue eyes.

They're Nathan-blue eyes.

My hand covers my mouth, stifling a gasp.

Nathan is on one knee.

Nathan. Where are his glasses?

The crowd is applauding, but I can barely hear them over the beating of my heart.

"Suzanna," he starts. He's miked up and loud.

But never too loud for me.

"There are so many things I could say to you, but the most important one of them is that I love you. You've brought so many things into my life. Fun, spontaneity, and at the risk of sounding corny, sunshine. I love you. Will you marry me?"

He opens that beautiful red box with the beautiful ring that I never let Ned put on my finger.

My heart is about to explode. "Yes. Yes, I will marry you."

He places the ring on my finger then stands. We kiss.

Of course, we kiss.

His arms feel like velvet around me. His lips can't kiss mine enough.

224

I know the crowd is going crazy, but I can't hear them.

Our kiss ends. I look into his eyes. "Where are your glasses?"

"I thought I'd give contacts a try. What do you think?"

"I think you better toss them in the trash. My guy wears glasses. And I love them just about as much as I love him."

He smiles. "Loving someone is about compromise. I wanted to show you I was flexible, willing to try something new."

"I love you just the way you are, Nathan. I only want you to be you."

He kisses me again.

I'm now truly the happiest girl in the world.

THE PARTY IS over, everyone is gone. Except for Nathan and me. We sit at a table among the mess. Empty glasses, crunched napkins, plates with food on them are being cleared away by the staff. But still we sit.

Nathan has put his glasses back on. Everything is right in the world. At least from my point of view. I look at my ring. "It's so beautiful."

"Like you."

"I can't believe this night. I know I've told you I wasn't going to let Ned propose, but then there you were. On your knee. I couldn't have imagined anything like this ever. Ever."

"You are my life. Everything I want in life is sitting right next to me."

Remembering the night I first met Nathan, I smile. "I still owe you money from the night we met."

He looks confused for a moment, then his face lights up with his smile. "I'm letting you off the hook. That's the best investment I've ever made."

I didn't know hearts could love this much. "I can't wait to marry you, Mr. Parks. Suzanna Parks. Has a nice ring to it. And Suzanna has a nice ring." I can't quit looking at my beautiful engagement ring.

"I see no reason to wait. Besides, I hear you might need a place to live."

"What?"

"According to your dad, your mom really likes your place. And she might want to move here. Only if she could have your place, though."

Mom is thinking about what I said. That makes me happy. "You sure do know a lot about my family."

Nathan has a sly look. "She might have a roommate, too. Your dad. I'm going to help him with a financial plan."

"Nathan, how is all of this working out? I feel like I'm in a dream. And I don't want to wake up."

"You are my dream. They are talking a double wedding. How do you feel about that?"

Wrapping my head around this love I feel is almost too much. It's unreal. Yet I know it's very real.

And perfect. "I just want to feel your lips on mine. Forever."

As his lips meet mine, they say one word.

Forever.

The End

Dear Reader,

Ah! Another Love Atlanta Style books is finished. Suzanna was so fun to write as she does things I would never do. She's crazy fun and spontaneous. Her wild spirit and boldness brought her many troubles, but of course it's all well in the end.

Many thanks to my editor, Emily Sewell. Always amazing! My mom, Jill Vaughan for the read throughs. Missy Tippens reigns me in in all the right places.

Riley's story is next!

I'm looking forward to writing her story. Girl next door meets savvy businessman.

To my ever supportive family—I love you.

And to my husband, Lenny, who always shows me what true love really is.

Thank you!

I appreciate each and every person who read the stories that find their way out of my head and into a book.

Lindi P.

Other books by Lindi Peterson

Love Atlanta Style Book 1
Uptown Heiress

The Wedding Dress Collection
The Little Black Wedding Dress

Richness in Faith Trilogy
Rich in Love

Rich in Hope

Rich in Faith

Summer's Song

Her Best Catch

Made in the USA
Lexington, KY
21 April 2017